SACRED CROSSROADS

THE PATH APPEARS WHEN YOU TAKE THE FIRST STEP.

MITCH RUSSO

MELBENDIUM
PRESS

CONTENTS

1

THE WELL-LIT PATHWAY

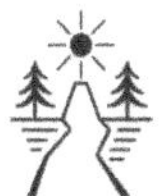

Noble Manning had built his life as his father had taught him: methodically, precisely, and with unwavering certainty.

Every morning at precisely six forty-five, he unlocked the heavy oak door of Manning's Hardware. The brass key, worn smooth by three generations of Manning hands, still turned with the same satisfying click.

The perfectly balanced slab of wood, metal, and trust glided smoothly as it opened on ancient brass hinges, just as his father had done for thirty years before him and his grandfather before that.

Manning's Hardware was the oldest store in Cedar Springs, Massachusetts, but it was also something more; it was its heart. Founded by Noble's grandfather in 1902, when Cedar Springs was barely more than a crossroads, the store had survived two world wars, the Great Depression, and the rise of big-box retailers.

The ledgers, kept meticulously by three generations of Mannings, from his grandfather's founding entries in 1902,

I

through his father's precise records, to Noble's own careful accounting, were the history of more than just transactions; they recorded the growth of Cedar Springs itself, one nail, one page at a time.

Their pages fluttered with a subtle energy as Noble turned them, each column of numbers pulsing with hidden frequencies. Between the careful accounting, other patterns emerged: his grandfather's notations about matching tools to their users, his father's observations of shadows that moved against the natural flow of light. These were memory nodes in a vast network of accumulated truth, waiting for the right resonance to activate, but Noble couldn't quite decode what was right there, right in front of him, waiting to be revealed.

From above the city, he could see most of Cedar Springs from the wraparound porch of his restored Victorian home. This was the same home his father had pointed out countless times during Noble's childhood, saying, "That's what success looks like, son."

From his vantage point, Cedar Springs revealed itself in layers of memory, each streetlight illuminating space and time. The cedar grove stood like silent servers, processing centuries of data through root networks that predated colonial paths. The springs beneath the town hall pulsed with liquid memory, their never-freezing waters carrying information too ancient for modern instruments to read. However, Noble was not yet fully aware of the spectrum of its history and patterns embedded in the environment; he felt them but couldn't see them.

Even at dusk, when shadows lengthened between the old maple trees, the streetlights would flicker on at exactly the right moment, keeping the darkness at bay.

That's how Noble liked things.

Predictable. Manageable. Under control. Just like his childhood.

He remembered watching other families at church picnics and town festivals thirty-five years ago, how some mothers would sweep their children into spontaneous hugs, how some fathers would throw an arm around their sons' shoulders or ruffle their hair.

The Manning way was different. "Dignity," his father would say, straightening Noble's already-straight tie. "Structure builds character," his mother would add, checking that his part was perfectly aligned.

Instead of bedtime stories, young Noble received lessons in inventory management from his father, Thomas, who had learned the same rigid lessons from Noble's grandfather in the store's early days.

While other kids played catch in their backyards, he learned how to stack lumber to maximize retail space. "This is your inheritance," his father would say, walking the impeccably organized aisles.

"Every nail, every bolt, every piece of advice we give our customers… it all matters."

And it did matter. The hardware store had put Noble through college in the early '80s and had funded his early years as a new graduate, just as it had supported his father's generation through the lean years after the war. Three generations of

hard work and dedication had made the Mannings a corner-
stone of Cedar Springs society.

If the price was a childhood short on hugs but long on responsibility lectures, that was just good business.

Cedar Springs held its secrets in layers, like the limestone
bedrock that cradled its mysterious springs. Noble could trace
the three ancient valleys that converged beneath the town
from his Victorian home's wraparound porch, their paths still
visible in the way the streets curved and shadows fell. The
cedar grove stood sentinel at the edge of town, with trees
older than memory, maintaining their immortal vigil. Noble
had learned early not to question why they remained green
year-round or why modern surveying equipment failed near
the intersection of Pine and Main.

Thomas Manning Sr., his grandfather, discovered this place in
1902, describing it as "a compelling necessity" that drew him
away from more profitable opportunities in nearby Marl-
borough.

Standing at the convergence of three colonial trading routes,
Thomas felt something that defied his practical nature, a resonance in the soil, an echo of older ways of knowing. He built
Manning's Hardware precisely at this intersection, although
he never explained why the location warranted such
exactness.

The town grew around the store, much like rings on a tree,
each layer adding its own unique story. The springs that gave
the city its name emerged from ancient limestone beneath the
town hall. Their waters carried mineral traces that no geolo-
gist had successfully identified. These springs never froze in
winter; sometimes, their surfaces would ripple without wind
or cause in the deepest hours of the night.

THE INVENTORY SHEETS blurred before Noble's tired eyes. After six hours of counting, the numbers still refused to balance: forty-seven hammers on the shelves, forty-five in the system. Twelve fewer boxes of nails than recorded, yet he hadn't sold any in that size for weeks.

Frustration drove him to the back corner, where the oldest tools were displayed. He'd check every item himself if necessary.

Noble jerked back in surprise as his hand brushed against an ancient Prybar, at the bottom rear of a dusty shelf, which his grandfather had stocked in 1902. The metal was almost hot despite the store's evening chill. He touched it again, more deliberately this time, feeling tiny vibrations like a distant humming. The longer he held it, the more he saw the different lives it had touched and felt their heart ebb through the moment.

A shadow moved in his peripheral vision, stretching across the floor against the direction of the overhead lights. It reminded him of something he'd tried to forget: his father standing in this exact spot after closing, head tilted as if straining to hear something.

"Your dad always said you had to listen when the store was empty," Jenny commented.

"It's just settling," Noble said automatically. "Old buildings make sounds."

"Is that why your grandfather insisted on using cedar from the grove for the frame? For the acoustics?" Her tone was gentle but challenging. "Or why certain tools feel different depending on where they're stored?"

Noble's hand still rested on the prybar, which now seemed to pulse with a rhythm like a heartbeat. He'd cataloged thousands of items over decades, measured every shelf to the quarter-inch, and tracked every sale to the penny. But he'd never allowed himself to measure this: the way certain spots in the store felt different, how shadows moved independently of light, how his father would stand motionless after closing hours.

"I don't know what you're talking about," he said, withdrawing his hand even as the prybar seemed reluctant to let him go.

"Trying to change the subject, "where's the Phillips-head display?" Noble muttered, scanning the aisle where it should have been.

"Third shelf, east wall," Jenny called from the register. "Again."

Noble frowned. He'd reorganized that section just yesterday, logically arranging the screwdrivers by the power tools. Yet here they were, migrated overnight to their old location.

He knelt to gather them, pausing when he noticed the warmth radiating from the metal. In April, in an unheated section of the store.

"They like it there," Jenny said, suddenly beside him. "Tools don't have preferences," Noble replied automatically.

"Maybe not in other hardware stores." Jenny picked up a screwdriver, which seemed to settle in her hand like an old friend. "Haven't you noticed? Anything we store near the center beam feels warm by morning. Anything hung on the north wall casts shadows that move... differently."

Noble had noticed, of course, for decades. He'd blamed heating vents, light angles, faulty inventory counts, anything but the obvious.

"It's just..." he began.

"Physics?" Jenny smiled. "Maybe so. Just not the kind they taught in school."

She placed the screwdriver back on the shelf. Neither commented when it rotated slightly to align with an invisible axis that pointed directly to the spot where three ancient trading routes had once converged.

Another Day Comes to a Close

Jenny caught Noble's eye from the register, where she was finishing her evening count. She had been part of Manning's Hardware longer than anyone else, carrying on her grandmother, Rosa's, legacy since she started working there as a teenager in the early '90s. Noble remembered the day she'd first walked in, seventeen and determined: her grandmother's medical bills clutched in one hand and hope in the other.

Jenny Martinez grew up between two worlds: Rosa's evening stories and her mother, Carmen's morning silence. Carmen, Rosa's daughter, cleaned rooms at the Cedar Springs Lodge before dawn and waited tables at Murphy's Diner until closing. She spoke little about the thirty years Rosa worked at Manning's Hardware, the three decades when her mother became Cedar Springs' keeper of unspoken wisdom.

"Mami saw too much," Carmen would say when Jenny asked about Rosa's time at the store. "Those Manning men, they let her arrange things her way because it worked. But working with spirits, with the old ways... it cost her. Made her different."

Rosa had raised Jenny while Carmen worked. In Rosa's kitchen, surrounded by herbs that grew according to the lunar cycles and pictures of the hardware store's early days, Jenny learned about the gift that ran in their bloodline. Rosa called it "el don de ordenar" - the gift of arranging. Not organizing by logic, but by the hidden relationships between objects and their purposes.

"Your great-grandmother in Guadalajara had this gift," Rosa explained in Spanish, her fingers tracing patterns on the worn kitchen table. "She could walk into any home and sense how furniture wanted to be placed for healing to occur. I brought this knowing to Manning's Hardware when I was young and desperate."

Jenny absorbed these lessons while sorting Rosa's button collection. Her small fingers moved automatically, creating patterns based on texture, temperature, and something deeper she could not name. Rosa watched approvingly.

"Thomas Manning Senior hired me because no one else would," Rosa continued. "A Mexican widow with a baby. But the store called to me. The tools needed a proper arrangement. The customers needed guidance on what would serve their true purposes."

At twelve, Jenny began accompanying Rosa to Manning's Hardware on Saturdays. She watched her grandmother move through the aisles with fluid purpose, touching certain items, relocating others. Customers would enter seeking one thing and leave with exactly what they needed, though often different from what they had requested.

"The store taught me as much as I taught it," Rosa explained. "Manning men build good systems. They measure carefully, track everything. My job was to help their systems breathe, to let intuition flow through their order."

When Rosa grew too frail for full-time work, she trained Jenny to see what she saw. Together, they would sit in Rosa's kitchen after school, with Jenny describing how each room in their house felt and what changes would improve its flow. Rosa nodded as Jenny's gift emerged naturally.

"Your mother fights this inheritance because she associates it with struggle," Rosa said. "She watched me work extra hours to support us both. She saw neighbors whisper about the Mexican woman who talked to tools. But you will find different ways to use this gift. Ways that honor both worlds."

At seventeen, when Rosa's medical bills mounted and Carmen's wages fell short, Jenny knew where to apply. The faded help-wanted sign at Manning's Hardware had hung unanswered for weeks. Other teenagers avoided the dusty store with its weird older owner and mysterious organizational systems.

Jenny walked through those familiar doors carrying her grandmother's training and her own fierce intelligence. She understood the store's rhythms through years of Saturday visits. She knew which corners held the most useful items, which displays guided customers toward decisions, and which arrangements Rosa had created to help Manning's Hardware serve its true purpose.

Noble Manning hired her because she demonstrated competence beyond her years. She balanced Rosa's intuitive arrangements with practical retail skills, translating the gift into language acceptable to modern commerce. What Noble saw as exceptional organizational ability was actually generations of inherited wisdom finding new expression.

Jenny became the bridge between Rosa's thirty years of service and Manning's Hardware's continuing evolution. She carried forward her gift while speaking the language of inventory management and customer service. In her hands, Rosa's legacy transformed into sustainable systems that honored both the gift and the business.

Customers never left empty-handed when Jenny worked the floor, though they sometimes purchased items entirely different from what they'd come seeking.

Jenny's fingers traced inventory patterns that defied conventional logic, leaving trails of remembered light in their wake. She moved through the aisles like a programmer navigating ancient code, each placement and adjustment made naturally, unconsciously, intuitively following protocols embedded in the store's very foundation. Noble watched her work, recognizing how her grandmother Rosa's wisdom had been encoded in these simple acts of arrangement.

The evening light slanted through the store windows, catching dust particles in the beams of light. Jenny's fingers moved over the register keys with quiet precision, each motion carrying the weight of experience. She had a way of making even the most mundane tasks feel purposeful, as if each number she tallied held meaning beyond its face value.

The register drawer closed with a familiar ring, but Jenny lingered over the final tally. Something about today's numbers felt charged with possibility, like tools waiting to be used for their true purpose. She'd always had this gift, this ability to sense when change was coming, though she rarely spoke of it.

Noble remembered the day Jenny applied for the job, seeing the tattered flyer taped to the store window week after week, which had gone unanswered. Still, Noble's father had hesitated to hire her.

"Too much whimsy," he'd said to his son, eyeing her flower-painted canvas shoes. "Customers need stability, not stories."

But then her smile melted two generations of Mannings on the spot, and they watched their world shift, knowing she deserved a chance. An odd choice, but with no one else applying, it was worth a shot.

Jenny had surprised them all.

Even then, with her vibrant thrift-store clothes and that ever-present book of poetry behind the counter, she'd had something special: a way of making everyone who walked through the door feel like they'd come home.

She knew every product and price, but more importantly, customers' names, their children's names, struggles, and triumphs. Where the Mannings offered precision, Jenny provided heart.

As the day drew to a close, the store held secrets in its stillness. Noble had noticed these moments more frequently lately when the familiar space seemed to breathe with its own rhythm. The tools and their shadows didn't quite match, and the ordinarily reassuring rows of inventory appeared to shimmer at the edges of his vision as if suggesting other arrangements beyond his understanding.

Jenny moved through these evening shadows with practiced ease, her movements flowing like water around stones. Where she saw shelves that needed straightening, she appeared to follow invisible patterns, touching certain items with deliberate care while passing others by. Noble never entirely understood her organizational system, yet customers always seemed to find exactly what they needed.

Noble stood quietly inside the front of Manning's Hardware and watched as Cedar Springs settled into dusk. Streetlights flickered on one by one, but they cast strange reflections tonight as if each pool of light seemed to hold stories rather than just illumination. Noble found himself thinking of old tales he'd heard as a child, whispered secrets about the town's hidden history, about people who could move between the ordinary moments of life.

The store's shadows lengthened with quiet precision, each one carrying encrypted fragments of past events: tools resonating with their true purpose, wood grain preserving the songs of forests, metal fittings holding echoes of every connection they'd ever formed. Noble had spent decades ignoring these patterns, instead filing them away as statistical anomalies. Lately, the logical classification systems of his certainty were screaming with anomalies, and subtle warnings were flashing at the edges of his consciousness.

The old wooden floors creaked their familiar patterns as Noble walked the aisles. Three generations of footsteps had worn energetic paths between the shelves. Sometimes, though he'd never admit it, he could swear the store felt different after hours, as if in the silence, he could sense conversations but couldn't quite hear.

As he walked back to his office to pick up his lunch box before closing for the night, he stopped to watch Jenny as she tidied up the register area. Noble had watched her over the years, balancing single motherhood with night classes, somehow keeping her light shining bright even through the darkest times.

Jenny's daughter Ruby was in college on a scholarship her mom had fought for with the same quiet determination she brought to everything.

The store had been her anchor through everything: her divorce, her mother's passing, and those lean years when she'd worked double shifts to keep food on her table. She'd turned down better-paying jobs at the new hardware chains in neighboring towns.

"Manning's is family," she'd always say, though Noble sometimes wondered if she knew more about family than he did.

Jenny was right behind Noble as he reached for his key to lock the front door as they left for the evening. "Sarah called again," she said softly, her voice carrying the weight of shared history.

Noble and Eleanor's daughter, Sarah, had the spitfire of her mom and the sensibilities of her dad. Jenny had known Sarah since birth and was the one to hold her through her first heartbreak and secretly support her dreams when Noble's practical concerns got in the way. Sarah had left Cedar Springs at twenty-three, fresh out of college and reeling from her mother's death the year before. Now, twelve years later, she'd built a life in Seattle as a curator at a small gallery specializing in photographs that captured moments between moments, as Eleanor used to say.

In many ways, Jenny had bridged the gap between Noble's structured world and his daughter's yearning for something more.

Jenny tucked a strand of silver-streaked hair behind her ear, a habit she'd had since high school. The wild colors were gone now, but that spark in her eyes, hinting at something deeper than daylight understanding, remained.

"She reminds me of my grandmother, you know? That same look in her eyes when she used to tell us stories about the Night Walkers and wisdom keepers," Jenny said.

Noble felt that familiar tightness in his chest. Jenny's grandmother had been Cedar Springs' unofficial storyteller, weaving tales that seemed to blur the line between reality and something else. She'd watch over the neighborhood children after school and entertain them with stories of a different world, now gone but never forgotten.

She and Jenny, among them, tell stories about people who learned to walk between worlds and who found their way after losing it first. Beautiful nonsense, his father would have said.

But Jenny had absorbed every word, and sometimes Noble caught glimpses of that ancient wisdom in how she handled troubled customers or soothed conflicts with a few well-chosen words.

Lately, something felt different.

The following day, as usual, Jenny was the first to arrive. She started the coffeepot she'd set up the night before, flipped on the lights, and turned up the heat. She knew that Noble would soon arrive, and it would be time for the day to begin with new and old customers seeking more than just tools.

Noble took pride in his morning inventory routine. Each item was in its designated place, and quantities were tracked down to the last washer.

Noble organized his morning in a way that mirrored his father's habits. His coat hung precisely where his dad's had hung. He made sure the coffee was measured to the exact scoop, and the ledgers were arranged at perfect angles on his desk.

In those stillest moments before the doors opened, Noble would linger over the inventory sheets, haunted by an inexplicable sense that the careful columns of numbers were somehow incomplete, like a conversation in which the most important words remained unsaid.

Lately, however, something had shifted in these familiar rituals. Nothing he could quantify, just a nagging sense that his careful measurements were missing something essential.

He found himself lingering over specific objects: a brass fitting that felt surprisingly warm in his hand, a roll of copper wire that seemed to softly vibrate as if connected to something significant beneath his fingers. At one point, he caught himself staring at his grandfather's old yardstick mounted behind the counter, pondering why its worn gradations revealed more to him than just inches.

These moments unsettled him precisely because they defied his lifelong devotion to the measurable. He dealt with them as he handled any anomaly, noting them briefly in his mental ledger before filing them under "inventory discrepancies." Yet they persisted, like equations that refused to balance, their variables shifting beyond his understanding.

Jenny announced that Frank's lumber had been cut, measured, and stacked on the loading dock out back, which brought him back to the reality of the store and his day.

The day was already underway with customers and phone calls, always urgent, and most handled effortlessly, leaving a sense of accomplishment knowing one more person was left satisfied.

The afternoon shadows lengthened across the store's wooden floors, each beam of fading sunlight carrying fragments of memory that seemed to lodge themselves in the grain of the floorboards. Noble had walked these aisles for thirty-five years, yet lately, they felt deeper, as if the space between shelves held more than just distance. He turned the corner with a frown, and Jenny smiled at him.

"Different," she said, watching him. "Not worse, just different." Her words carried an echo of understanding that made Noble's chest tighten.

How did she always seem to name the things he was afraid to acknowledge and to verbalize the thoughts he couldn't quite articulate?

He thought as he walked the aisles, nudging inventory items back into their precise locations.

The morning inventory sheets scattered across his desk revealed confusing discrepancies. Tools migrated between shelves overnight; quantities shifted like quantum variables refusing to be measured.

His carefully maintained ledger lay open before him, but he couldn't bring himself to record these aberrations. Instead, he straightened the papers for the third time, adjusting their angles to perfect right degrees, as if proper alignment could restore the old reality.

ANOTHER TUESDAY: serving customers, managing deliveries, facing challenges, and achieving some profits had come to a close.

Through the store windows, Cedar Springs transformed in the gathering dusk. The streetlights created pools of illumination that didn't quite touch the ground, hanging instead like doorways into different dimensions. Standing there silently observing the empty streets, Noble remembered how Eleanor used to photograph the town at this hour, insisting that twilight revealed truths behind the shadows that daylight couldn't capture.

Eleanor Hartwell had arrived in Cedar Springs carrying a battered camera case and eyes that saw too much. She'd grown up in Portland, daughter of an insurance adjuster who measured loss in dollars and a mom who was a librarian cataloguing stories by the Dewey Decimal System. Both parents lived comfortably within boundaries: claims processed, books shelved, reality contained.

Eleanor felt out of place at fourteen when her high school photography class developed its first rolls of black-and-white film. While her classmates captured standard portraits and landscape compositions, Eleanor's negatives showed something different: layers that other cameras missed - shadows cast by trees, which contained the shapes of birds not present when she pressed the shutter. Empty park benches held the impressions of conversations yet to happen.

Her photography teacher, Mrs. Brennan, studied Eleanor's prints with growing concern. "These are double exposures," she said, examining images that clearly showed single shots. "Your camera must have a light leak."

Eleanor tried different cameras. The results remained consistent. She learned to develop her own film in the basement darkroom her father built, spending hours watching images emerge from the darkness. Each photograph revealed more than the eye had seen: moments between moments, possibilities hiding in ordinary scenes.

Her parents worried. Eleanor spent increasing hours alone with her camera. She photographed empty rooms that her lens revealed as full of activity, vacant lots that bloomed with structures not yet built. Her grades suffered as she pursued visions her teachers dismissed as artistic pretension.

At seventeen, Eleanor's photographs began showing people in states of transformation. A grocery clerk surrounded by light that suggested healing gifts. A mechanic whose hands glowed with the ability to repair more than engines. She realized her camera captured what people could become, not just what they appeared to be.

The discovery both thrilled and terrified her. Eleanor understood she possessed something beyond artistic talent. Her photographs revealed truth in ways that made others uncomfortable. Friends stopped asking to see her work. Teachers disapproved, telling her parents she would not likely be successful, since who would want what she produced?

After graduation, Eleanor wandered the Pacific Northwest with her camera. But the results were always the same: finding the space between what was and what could be. She photographed loggers who swore the tales of their ancestors, waitresses who served hope alongside coffee, and dentists who could fix cavities and broken hearts.

In 1987, a story assignment brought her to Cedar Springs, MA, to document small-town hardware stores for a regional magazine. She entered Manning's Hardware, expecting to capture a quaint slice of Americana. Instead, her camera revealed layers of magic she'd never encountered: tools that chose their owners, wood that whispered its preferred uses, a young man behind the counter who glowed with inherited gifts he refused to acknowledge.

Noble Manning appeared in her viewfinder, surrounded by golden light, his hands touching inventory that responded to his presence despite his determined blindness to the connection. Eleanor spent an hour photographing him, arranging displays, watching through her lens as tools migrated toward their intended purposes whenever he touched them.

When she showed him the contact sheets, Noble laughed off the strange effects as lighting tricks and chemical accidents. But Eleanor saw recognition flicker in his eyes before he dismissed what her camera had captured.

"You see it too," she said softly. "The way things respond to you. The way the store feels different when you're working in it."

Noble's defensive response told Eleanor everything she needed to know. Here was someone whose gift ran as deep as hers but who'd learned to fear rather than embrace it.

The day had ended, and it was time to close up. As he flipped off the interior lights, the old brass key felt unusually warm, hanging against his chest as he moved to check the window displays. Each item he touched seemed alive with story: hammers that bore the echo of every nail, measuring tapes that measured futures as readily as walls, and paint cans cradling colors that carried memory into possibility.

"Your father used to see it too," Jenny said softly, arranging items with subtle, purposeful movements. "Especially at this time of day. He'd stand right there, pretending to check inventory, but really..." She let the words trail off, her hands continuing their mysterious choreography among the tools.

Noble wanted to dismiss her words and retreat into the comfort of his evening routine. However, the shadows continued to shift at the corners of his vision, and he could have sworn he heard the sound of his father's old ledger pages turning in the back room, even though no wind stirred in the still air.

In those precisely measured aisles of the hardware store, and the shadows between them felt deeper than ever, with things shifting in ways he chose to ignore.

The air between the shelves seemed to thicken as the accumulated vibrations of decades of transactions encoded themselves into the store's invisible layers. Noble felt this most strongly near the original cedar beams, where his grandfather had first established the hardware store's foundation. Something within the wood's matrix was shifting, arranging itself, preparing to activate programs that had lain dormant for generations.

He couldn't quite pinpoint it, so he did what he often did with anything that didn't align with his patterns. He pushed it aside and concentrated on what he could manage.

As the key to Manning's Hardware clicked into place and the door swung shut behind him, Noble pondered the sun's orange, reddish glow as he wrapped up another day's routine.

Tomorrow would mirror every other Friday: inventory in the morning, a Chamber of Commerce lunch meeting at noon, and appointments with suppliers in the afternoon.

Everything was in its place, and everything was on track.

Like the springs that never froze and the cedars that never died, Manning's Hardware maintained its own strange constancy. Noble had dedicated his life to measuring the measurable and containing what could be contained. But lately, the boundaries were growing thinner, like twilight shadows stretching toward dawn.

And so it was: a good family, strong values, and a local business. The Mannings were pillars of the community for three generations, as demonstrated over the years.

But there was a hidden side to Thomas Manning, Sr. Besides being the family's patriarch, he kept the family secrets, and maybe, just maybe, it was the time they were revealed.

2

WHEN THE LIGHT SHIFTS

Noble's phone rang at precisely 3:17 a.m. He knew the time because he'd been staring at his bedside clock for hours, haunted by memories he usually kept carefully filed away.

Earlier that evening, while locking up the store, he caught a glimpse of something in the backroom mirror. Just for a moment, he could have sworn he saw Eleanor there, camera in hand, watching him as he stood there, among all the secrets waiting to be revealed. Her photography, that passion, was one of the many things he loved most about her.

She had tried for three years to show Noble what her camera revealed about him, about the store, about Cedar Springs itself. She would spread contact sheets across their kitchen table, pointing to images where his shadow cast light instead of darkness, where his hands left traces of energy on tools he'd touched.

"Look at this one," she'd say, her voice patient despite repeated rejections. "You're arranging lumber, but see how the wood grain aligns itself after you walk past? This isn't a coincidence, Noble."

Noble would glance at the photographs and return to his ledgers. "Interesting effects," he'd say, his tone suggesting anything but interest. "Must be something about the lighting in the store."

He tried so hard to unsee what was right there in front of him. It became harder still with each roll of film Eleanor developed. She saw wonder everywhere: in how customers found exactly what they needed in Noble's carefully organized aisles, in how Rosa's arrangements seemed to guide people toward discoveries they hadn't known they were seeking, in how the store itself seemed to breathe with purpose.

Noble saw efficient inventory management and customer service. Nothing more.

Eleanor's photographs grew increasingly desperate and revealing. She captured images of Cedar Springs' hidden nature: the bakery where bread told stories of future families, the garage where mechanical problems reflected emotional ones, the print shop where words held power beyond their meaning. Each photograph was an attempt to show Noble the magical world surrounding them both.

The night Sarah was born, Eleanor's camera malfunctioned for the first time in twenty years. Every photograph she took in the hospital showed only what was visible to the naked eye. No auras, no possibilities, no layers of meaning. Just a tired woman holding her newborn daughter.

"Maybe it's broken," Noble suggested, relief evident in his voice. "You've been pushing that old camera pretty hard."

Eleanor sensed something else - a transfer of sorts - her daughter's inheritance, flowing from her into the tiny girl sleeping against her chest. Sarah would grow up seeing what Eleanor saw, carrying forward the sight gift that the family had suppressed for generations.

The camera resumed its magical function when they brought Sarah home to Manning's Hardware. The first photograph Eleanor took of her daughter showed the infant surrounded by light that would never fade, holding potential that would reshape their world.

Noble looked at the image and saw only his sleeping child. Eleanor saw the future keeper of visions, the bridge between his practical world and her magical one.

She stopped trying to convince him after that night. Instead, Eleanor focused on documenting Sarah's growing gift, creating a visual record of transformation that Noble might someday understand. Her camera became a patient teacher, capturing truth for eyes that might eventually learn to see.

He picked up the receiver after the first ring. "Dad?"

Sarah's voice carried the weight of thirteen years spent trying to build a life where magic couldn't find her. She'd thrown herself into the academic world of art curation, analyzing fine art photographs while pretending not to see the transformations happening around her.

But every exhibition she curated seemed to draw people seeking something between the images, just as her mother's photographs had. Even three thousand miles away, she couldn't escape what she was.

Noble's hand trembled as he reached for the bedside lamp. Sweat beaded on his forehead despite the cool night air. Something in Sarah's tone, a certainty he'd last heard in Eleanor's voice, made his chest tighten.

"What's wrong?" he asked. Switching on the light revealed his perfectly ordered room, with everything in its assigned place, but it did not comfort him for what was coming.

"Grandma's key is glowing."

Noble gripped the phone harder, his knuckles white, doing what he'd always done when faced with the unexplainable: search for reasonable explanations like a man checking his wallet repeatedly for a missing receipt.

But this time, the familiar comfort of denial slipped through his fingers like loose change.

Sarah continued.

"The shadows are wrong, Dad. They're shifting when they shouldn't. And the key... It's not reflecting light. It's producing it. Like Mom's photographs used to do."

Noble sat still and remembered the first time he saw it, not saying a word.

The old brass key that hung in his father's office was a family artifact passed down from Noble's grandfather, who founded the store in 1902, to his father Thomas, who recognized Rosa's gift in 1942, and then finally to Noble himself.

He remembered the day Rosa Martinez first noticed it when she started working at the store. While Rosa was in conversation with Grandpa Manning, she stopped mid-sentence, her eyes fixed on the key as if it were speaking to her.

"That key," Rosa said in her accented English, "has been waiting."

His grandfather, usually quick to dismiss anything that couldn't be measured, had just nodded.

Many years later, Grandma Manning gave Sarah the key on her sixteenth birthday. "Some things choose their keepers," she said, despite Grandpa's objections. But she knew Sarah was the next keeper, and it was time to pass on the key. She understood it had a greater purpose and had been waiting for this day to come.

Now deep in reverie, Noble was there that day with Eleanor, as her camera caught subtle shifting lights around Sarah as she held the key for the first time.

"Dad, are you there?" Sarah asked after a long silence.

"That's not possible," he said, but even as the words left his mouth, he remembered finding Eleanor's last roll of film after the accident.

Photos of empty meadows, except... had they been empty?

In one, he'd caught a glimpse of something, shapes like horses made of morning mist, visible only when he wasn't quite looking at them. He marveled at their beauty and simplicity, knowing that Eleanor saw something, and he wished he could, too.

The words came automatically, his father's voice in his head. Noble reached for his leather-bound ledger, where he recorded the day's receipts on the nightstand, fingers seeking comfort in its precise columns and measurable facts. But the pages felt strange under his touch, as if the numbers were trying to tell him something other than facts.

"I know what you're thinking, Dad. That I'm being dramatic again or having another 'phase.' But something's happening in Cedar Springs. Have you looked at the store lately? Really looked?"

He had. Though he'd never say it aloud, the shadows felt different lately.

Noble's mind raced through the subtle changes he'd been noticing over the past several months but had purposely ignored. The inventory discrepancies were growing more frequent; tools that seemed warmer to the touch than they should have been, and reflections in the store that lingered after the lights were turned off. Just last week, Mrs. Chen had mentioned hearing whispers by the seed bins near the gardening tools, and Jack Thompson swore his wood was "singing" when he cut it. Even Jenny had become more like her grandmother lately, spending more time arranging tools in patterns that defied conventional organization but somehow made sense to customers.

Rosa had predicted this. On her deathbed seven years ago, she had gripped Noble's hand with surprising strength and whispered, "When the thresholds thin and the keys remember their purpose… be ready."

He'd dismissed it as the ramblings of a dying woman. But Rosa had also said something else… that it would happen in the spring of this year, when "three ancient paths cross again in the sky." Noble thought he had seen a strange astronomical alignment in the newspaper just the day before; a rare config-uration the article called a "celestial crossroads," visible only once every forty-nine years.

The timing was exactly as Rosa had foretold.

Deeper, more dimensional somehow. Last week, he'd found Rosa's old ledger, where she'd recorded stories about the store and their customers, which tools had built which houses, which gardens had grown from seeds bought in which seasons. His father had called it her "fairy tale book" but had never thrown it away.

Sarah started recalling her many conversations with Jenny and the sense of awe and truth she felt from every one of them. "Jenny's grandmother, Rosa, used to say…" she said…

"Jenny's grandmother said many things," Noble cut in, without his usual dismissiveness.

The late hour had softened something in him. He remembered sitting in Rosa's kitchen as a boy while she taught Jenny the old ways of seeing. Eleanor would often be there before they were married, her artist's eyes drinking every word.

"She said the Night Walkers would return when needed. When the town needed to remember something it had forgotten." Sarah paused.

"Dad, the key isn't the only thing that's changed. I'm coming home."

The words hung in the air like visible breath on a cold morning. Sarah hadn't called Manning's Hardware "home" since she left for college thirteen years ago. She left because she knew it wasn't her time and the store wasn't ready for the transformation ahead, but she knew the time would come someday, as she's known all along the secrets of Manning's Hardware.

Hidden in her mom's journals, full of descriptions of seemingly impossible things, lights coming from trees, songs in old tools, stories in the grain of wood. These confirmed what she had believed all along.

Noble, after a period of awkward silence, "It's the middle of the night?" he asked, reflecting on practicality. "We can talk about this in the morning."

"Dad," Her voice held that same strange clarity. "By morning, it will be too late. Could you do something for me? Go to the store. Now. And take Jenny with you."

"Jenny? Why would I…"

"Because she sees what you don't. She always has."

The line went dead, leaving Noble in his too-bright room with his too-ordered thoughts scattering like startled birds.

Jenny's relationship with magic was different from Sarah's. While Sarah had inherited her gift through the Manning bloodline, Jenny had acquired it out of necessity and loss.

Her mother, born just before Rosa arrived at Manning's in '42, had given up the old ways after Jenny's father left them.

However, that rejection only drew Jenny closer to her grandmother, as she spent evenings in Rosa's kitchen. At the same time, her mother worked double shifts, learning to read the truth in ordinary things, while Rosa immersed Jenny in the knowings of her ancestors.

"Your mother thinks that hiding from magic will shield you," Rosa would say, teaching Jenny to feel the stories in worn wood and rusted metal. "But magic seeks out those who need it most." Jenny had understood even back then that her mother's blindness came from pain, not disbelief.

Jenny sat at Rosa's kitchen table, the exact spot where her grandmother had taught her to feel stories from the unseen world. The house still held Rosa's presence seven years after her death: herbs dried in careful bundles, ceramic bowls that had stirred more than ingredients, wooden spoons worn smooth by decades of use.

The crystals hanging in the window had been chiming since sunset. Rosa had placed them there in 1995, the year Jenny started working at Manning's Hardware full-time. "They sing when the barriers grow thin," Rosa had explained.

Jenny opened Rosa's personal ledger, distinct from the store records. These pages held her grandmother's observations about Cedar Springs, about the Manning family, about the gift that had shaped both their lives. Her fingers found an entry dated three months before Rosa's death:

"Jenny carries the wisdom blood, but she also carries something new. Her struggle with single motherhood, her nights studying while Ruby slept, her fierce determination to build stability - these experiences forge the strength and the gift needed to survive in the modern world. When the awakening comes, she will know how to ground visions in practical reality."

Jenny touched her chest, feeling the phantom weight of infant Ruby against her shoulder during those long nights when colicky crying mixed with textbook reading. She had learned to balance Rosa's intuitive teachings with business courses taken at the community college after Ruby went to bed. The combination had made her invaluable to Noble, though he never understood why her organizational methods worked better than conventional systems.

Ruby stirred in her upstairs bedroom. At twenty-three, she was finishing her physics PhD, but she still responded to Cedar Springs when it called to her in dreams. Jenny felt the familiar pull across three generations: Rosa's ancient knowing, her own ability to build bridges, and Ruby's scientific vision that would someday unlock quantum possibilities.

STILL SITTING at her grandmother's old kitchen table, Rosa's worn journal open before her. She'd been awake since midnight when the crystals in her windows started chiming without wind. The sound had pulled her from dreams of the store as it used to be when Rosa worked there.

Her fingers traced her grandmother's elegant script: "The Manning store holds more than just hardware. It contains the memory of every dream, every home created, and every garden grown from its tools and seeds. Places like this probably exist all over the world, crossroads where differing realities meet. But only some cross over to the other side."

Sitting still, she watched with fascination as the journal's pages turned by themselves, settling on an entry from 1943, the year after Rosa had started working at Manning's.

"Today, young Thomas Manning saw the way some tools carry light and others hold shadows. He tries to ignore what is clearly happening and hide behind his ledgers and numbers, but he possesses the old sight, just like his father before him. The key recognized him as it will recognize others when the time comes."

Noble recalled the stories about his father, Thomas Manning, who offered Rosa a job in 1942 when no one else would employ a young Mexican widow. This decision would shape the store and impact the entire town's destiny. He remembered how he'd let her organize tools, following patterns only she could see.

Everyone claimed it was charity, but Jenny's grandmother knew better. "Thomas Manning understands the truth of things," Rosa wrote about Noble's father. "He recognizes that this place is more than just a store. It's a crossing point where the visible and invisible worlds touch. The Mannings have been guardians without knowing it, keeping the door open by helping people build, repair, and create their dreams."

But Thomas Manning, Sr., saw more than he was given credit for. He saw the possibilities and believed that many of them were good. He needed to preserve this place in the universe where such a place could exist, and so he did quietly, without a word to anyone. But Rosa knew; he was sure of that.

The crystals chimed again, and Jenny felt a familiar presence; her grandmother's energy, lingering in this house after all these years. Rosa had known this night would come. She'd prepared Jenny for it, teaching her the old ways while showing her how to work a cash register, track inventory, and bridge the worlds of practical commerce and ancient wisdom.

Jenny thought of Eleanor then: the beautiful, wild Eleanor who had the sight gift and saw the truth from the beginning. As she walked into Manning's Hardware twenty-five years ago with a camera full of photos and with eyes that could see past the veil of ordinary reality, he saw her.

Noble had fallen in love with her instantly, though he'd spent years trying to rationalize what she showed him through her photographs.

"She has the sight," Rosa had written. "And their child will have it, too. The key is already waiting for her."

The phone rang, startling Jenny from her memories. Noble's name glowed on the screen, just as she'd known it would.

"I've been waiting for your call," she answered.

"Sarah called," he said, his voice tight with controlled confusion.

"The key is glowing, isn't it?"

Jenny touched her grandmother's journal, feeling the pulse of old magic through its pages. The same magic that had drawn Rosa to Cedar Springs all those years ago, that had kept her at Manning's Hardware through decades of change.

"How did you know?"

"My grandmother's stories weren't just stories, Noble. You know that. You've always known that even if you couldn't let yourself believe it." She was already reaching for her coat. "I'll meet you at the store in twenty minutes."

"Jenny, this is ridiculous. It's the middle of the night."

"Yes," she said. "That's when it starts."

Jenny sat at her kitchen table, fingers tracing the worn edges of Rosa's ledger. The scent of chamomile tea, her grandmother's cure for sleepless nights, filled the small room. She'd known sleep wouldn't come tonight; the crystals in her window had been chiming since sunset, though no wind stirred the air.

She remembered the first time she'd noticed things others couldn't see. She'd been seven, helping Rosa stock shelves at Manning's. The tools had whispered to her, not in words exactly, but in feelings: which hammer belonged in which hands, which saw would build something meaningful.

She'd thought everyone could sense it until she mentioned it to her mother, who'd quickly shushed her. But Rosa smiled, took her small hand, and showed her how to listen deeper.

Eleanor had seen it, too. Jenny remembered watching her photograph the store after hours, capturing images of something beyond regular sight. They'd formed an unspoken alliance: the photographer, the stock girl, and Rosa, each understanding something Noble fought so hard to deny.

While searching for his father's old inventory lists, Noble found a leather-bound journal wedged between decades of dusty ledgers.

Inside, his father's precise handwriting from the post-war years gave way to hurried notes about a mysterious figure who walked the streets of Cedar Springs during the darkest hours. The dates matched the period when Rosa's influence on the store was strongest, throughout the 1950s and early '60s.

"He appears when change is near," one entry read.

"I've seen him three times now, always before moments when the store was in danger or when the magic drew closer. He carries tools that shift in shape within his apron, and his eyes hold landscapes I can't describe," his father noted.

Noble recognized the dates, marking a time when Cedar Springs stood at a crossroads. The last entry, written the night before his father's death, remained unfinished: "The Night

Walker came again. He says my son will need to understand what I never could. Now, the time approaches when measurement alone won't suffice. I should tell Noble about..."

Noble closed the journal, confused and in denial. His father had known all along; the truth was finally uncovered, preparing him for what was to come.

Years later, Jenny still arranged inventory by intention rather than category.

She'd seen his quick steps past shelves where shadows moved oddly and noticed how he avoided the backroom mirror that occasionally reflected moments instead of images.

Sitting in her kitchen, her tea had grown cold, and Jenny barely noticed. Her grandmother's ledger contained the true history of Manning's Hardware and Cedar Springs itself. Rosa had recorded what was sold and what was built: dreams, hopes, and new beginnings. Jenny continued this practice in her own way, matching specific tools to purpose.

"Soon," she whispered to the quiet kitchen. The crystals chimed in agreement, and she knew a key was waking up.

It was time to head over and meet Noble, knowing he couldn't take the next step alone.

In the middle of the night…

Noble got dressed despite his best intentions to be rational about all this nonsense; he didn't want to disappoint Jenny or Sarah.

Years of carefully buried memories surfaced like bodies rising through dark water. He remembered when Eleanor had stood in her darkroom, trying to show him the shapes that moved between the shadows in her photographs. "Look deeper," she said, her eyes bright with discovery. He smiled, called her his beautiful dreamer, and focused instead on next week's inventory.

His mind then resonated with his father's voice, sharp as winter wind: "Manning men deal in facts, son. Leave the stories to Rosa." But even as the words echoed, other memories pushed through.

One day long ago, he'd found his father standing motionless in the tool aisle, just staring at colors that danced without music. The night he'd caught him adding strange notes in the ledger margins, only to snap it shut when he noticed Noble watching.

The taste of copper filled his mouth as he remembered Sarah at seven, tugging his sleeve. "Daddy, why are the hammers singing?" Smiling, he sent her to help Jenny stock shelves rather than explaining that he had heard it, too. His father told him to ignore how the tools arranged themselves around his daughter's tiny hands.

For months now, Noble noticed more activity than usual, dismissing it as before, yet undeniable as the pace of events quickened,

Every unexplained noise he'd dismissed. Every odd reflection he'd refused to see twice. Every time, inventory numbers balanced even though the dollars didn't. His chest tightened with the weight of decades of denial.

Noble gripped the steering wheel of his ancient but well-maintained Volvo, the leather wheel cold against his palms. He could feel Eleanor's presence, her scent of lavender, her touch on his arm as he turned the ignition key, anticipating the usual sputter as the engine came to life.

The familiar route to Manning's Hardware felt like driving through a life he no longer recognized, even though nothing had visibly changed. Each landmark he'd once relied upon for navigation now seemed as unreliable as the plans he'd made before Eleanor's death, before Sarah left, and before certainty had turned into just another word for blindness.

Streetlights flickered as he passed, their usual steady glow wavering like his confidence in everything he'd built his life upon.

The dashboard clock read 3:32 a.m. Its pulsing green digits offered a momentary comfort until he noticed the numbers shimmering, as if trying to show him other times, other possibilities.

Cedar Springs slept, but not peacefully.

Shadows pooled too deeply between buildings, and the few lit windows he passed seemed to watch him. The smell of copper filled his nostrils, like fear, like change. His father's voice echoed: "Numbers don't lie, son. Trust what you can measure." But Sarah's words about the glowing key kept pace with his heartbeat.

The store's silhouette emerged from the darkness ahead. Noble had always taken pride in how it anchored the corner of Pine and Main, solid and predictable as sunrise. Tonight, though, the brick walls appeared to breathe in the moonlight. The windows, he could have sworn, held more than just reflections.

He pulled into his usual parking spot but cut the engine quickly. The silence pressed against his ears. Every cell in his body urged him to restart the car, drive home, and crawl back into his ordered world of ledgers and inventory counts. Instead, his hand moved to the car door handle, cold metal against clammy skin.

"It's just the store," he whispered to himself convincingly. But even his voice sounded different in the strange quiet, as if the words themselves knew better.

Each heartbeat brought a hint of what hung in the balance. If Sarah was right, if the key truly glowed with its own light, then everything he'd built his life around might not be as real as he thought... even the very fabric of Cedar Springs itself.

As he gazed through the windshield, he could see how the town's sleeping streets told their own story of the past. Each darkened storefront concealed its own magic, long suppressed beneath fluorescent lights and credit card readers.

Mrs. Chen's bread was always unique in ways he couldn't quite describe, with ingredients he could never have guessed. Jack Thompson's wood seemed to sing of forests long forgotten. If all of it connected to an awakening, it just might threaten the comfortable illusion of ordinary life.

If he walked into his store tonight and acknowledged what Sarah and Jenny had always seen, there would be no returning to spreadsheets and inventory counts. No more hiding behind his father's rigid certainty.

The cost of seeing would be the comfort of blindness.

But the price of turning away now… Noble's throat tightened as the truth settled into his bones. He thought of Sarah, holding a glowing key that belonged to a legacy he'd spent decades denying. Of Jenny, preserving Rosa's wisdom while he pretended not to notice. Of Eleanor, who'd died still trying to show him what existed between seconds and shadows.

The keys in his pocket seemed to grow heavier as if gathering the weight of choice. Noble had no idea that tonight would determine more than just his path; it would shape the town's destiny.

Noble could feel the pressure of generations watching. His grandfather, who'd first opened these doors; his father, who'd chosen ledgers over legends; and now Sarah, asking him to finally see what had always been there, which he had denied out of fear of the truth.

The brass key hummed against Noble's palm, its surface worn smooth by three generations of Manning hands. Sometimes, in the quietest moments before opening, he could swear he felt other mornings layered within this one: his father's precise movements and his grandfather's careful rituals. The key seemed to carry their memories like embedded code; each turn in the lock accessed data he wasn't quite ready to decode.

The store's windows flickered again, this time allowing Noble to catch glimpses of Cedar Springs' possible futures in their reflections.

In one, the town remained safely ordinary, its magic fading like morning mist until even the memory of wonder was lost. In another, something awakened, not just in Manning's Hardware, but in every shop, every home, and every heart that had forgotten how to see.

The store's brick facade rippled like water disturbed by unseen stones as he watched. Even the night air felt charged with potential, carrying scents of Eleanor's darkroom chemicals, Rosa's spiced tea, and something older... like time itself becoming tangible.

The night held its breath, waiting for Noble to make his choice.

Noble stepped out of his car into a night unlike any he had known in his sixty-three years. This could be the precise moment when certainty crumbled and possibility awakened... and it was about to begin.

JENNY'S dented Volkswagen served her well. It was old, reliable, and comfortable, but not overly comfortable. It connected her to her earlier memories of her mom owning a Volkswagen just like it, reminding her how she sat in the tiny back seat, humming to herself, as her mom did what she could to put food on the table and support them.

As she drove through the sleeping town, Jenny thought of Noble's daughter, Sarah, probably already returning to Cedar Springs. The key would have called her home, just as it had once called Eleanor.

Just as the store had called to Rosa, guiding her to this small town where hardware and magic mingled in the dusty corners and tool shadows.

Noble was already there when she arrived; he was standing under the streetlight, just standing there staring at the front door, looking more lost than she'd ever seen him.

For a moment, she saw him as her grandmother had described him in her journal: "A boy with ancient eyes, trying so hard to see the world only through his father's practical lens.

But the old knowing runs in his blood, whether he admits it
or not."

3

WHAT CAN'T BE MEASURED

J enny clicked off the ignition, and the air-cooled engine sputtered briefly. She tugged the reluctant door handle and stepped out. Watching Noble just standing there, not even noticing her as she arrived, she walked toward him, and then her hand gripped his arm.

"Steady," she whispered. "Remember why you are here."

The store key turned in the lock, but not with the familiar click Noble had known for thirty-five years. Instead, it resonated like a bell struck underwater, deep and strange, a tone that seemed to ripple through the bones of the building itself.

He nearly dropped the keyring as the vibration traveled up his arm, carrying visions of generations of Mannings unlocking this door, each time with their own hopes, fears, and understanding of what awaited. Terrified, he just stood there, hoping that he would have the courage to confront what had been there all his life.

"The first step is always the hardest," she said as she moved him into the store.

42

But Noble already felt as if he were standing outside of himself, observing from a distance as he moved without sensation. The pre-dawn air had shifted from its usual crisp clarity to something thicker, more inert, as if the space between moments had become tangible.

He counted his breaths, trying to impose mathematical certainty on a world rapidly becoming impossible to quantify.

The store's inventory system had been his fortress of order. Every item was categorized, measured, and accounted for in ledgers that stretched generations. But as they crossed the threshold, those careful measurements seemed to blur and shift.

The aisles he'd walked for thirty-five years seemed to stretch beyond their known dimensions, tools casting shadows that moved independently of any light source.

Noble's fingers instinctively reached for his pocket calculator, a habit formed from decades of morning inventory counts. But the familiar plastic felt wrong against his skin; it was too warm, as if it resisted the same reality as Noble. The digital display flickered randomly.

"The shadows," he whispered, his voice tight with controlled panic. "They're not... they shouldn't..." He knew that he could no longer ignore what he had worked so hard to dismiss before.

Jenny moved past him with the fluid grace she'd always possessed, but now her movement seemed more purposeful, as if she were following patterns visible only to her.

"Some things can't be measured in the usual ways," she said, Rosa's accent coloring her words more strongly than usual. "Some truths need different kinds of logic."

The store's awakening resonated with something more profound that lived in the marrow of his bones and the legacy of his blood.

"Your father knew," Jenny said softly, her hand trailing along the shelves that gleamed at her touch. "Just as his father knew before him. The Mannings were never merely shopkeepers, but you knew that, didn't you?" She turned to face him, Rosa's ancient wisdom burning in her eyes, and repeated her words:

"You are all guardians of a sacred crossroad, keepers of the places where ordinary people come to discover their extraordinary purpose and awaken to a greater mission."

The keys at Noble's chest seemed to pulse in harmony with this truth. For a moment, he hesitated and turned to leave, feeling overwhelmed all at once.

Without eye contact, he told Jenny, "It's all too much; I don't know how I can, I…"

As he turned, the sky outside began shifting from total darkness to the beginning of dawn, casting a glow on the street outside. Through the windows, Cedar Springs existed in multiple states: the sleeping town he'd always known and something else that waited behind the facade of normalcy like a dream waiting to be remembered.

"All those years," Noble whispered, memories shifting like tectonic plates.

"My father's insistence on precise organization, the careful cataloging of every transaction..." He touched the ancient ledger, feeling energy ripple through its pages. "I thought we were just tracking inventory. But no. We were... containing it? Directing it?"

"Protecting it," Jenny corrected. "Keeping the doorway open, even when you couldn't see where it led. Every generation of Mannings has served as anchor points, places where the practical and the possible could safely meet, preparing for the right moment: this moment when the dimensions between worlds would shift."

Reflecting on Manning's Hardware history, Jenny continued. "And each of you needed to reach your own vision of this place, nothing the past generation could or should share; you had to come to this point by yourself, just as your father and grandfather had."

Jenny gently moved him back to his original path to discover who he truly was, as if emerging from a deep sleep and seeing the world for the first time.

The store's shadows came alive with meaning, memory, and magic that had always lived in the spaces between mundane moments. Noble remembered his grandfather's careful measurements, his father's rigid systems, and his obsession with order as frameworks built to channel something vast and luminous; he remembered his father's words whispered to the empty shelves before him.

"Some doorways need keepers who remember what they're keeping. Who understands that some things can't be measured, only preserved."

Noble felt the weight of generations pressing against his consciousness, not just the Mannings but all the families who'd built Cedar Springs with tools that became instruments of transformation.

The pre-dawn air thickened with possibility, and Noble suddenly, as if plugged into a vast matrix, understood what

he'd been protecting all these years without realizing it…
until now.

"This place is a sacred junction where the ordinary world can safely remember its extraordinary nature," he murmured as if speaking to no one.

Noble touched the old brass key that had opened this door thousands of times in his father's hands.

"When my father would say, 'Manning's measures more than merchandise,' I always thought he meant customer service." A quiet laugh escaped him, half-wonder and half-regret. "But he was trying to tell me, wasn't he? In his way?"

"Each generation finds its way to pass on the truth," Jenny said. "Some through stories, some through secrets. Some through systems that look like ordinary business practices to all but those who need to know."

The weight of legacy settled around Noble's shoulders, feeling more like a burden than a birthright: he finally understood. "All these years," he whispered, "I thought I was preserving a family business. But we were preserving something far more essential, weren't we?"

Jenny's smile carried centuries of knowing. "You're standing at the edge of understanding what Manning's has always been. The question is, Noble… are you ready to step fully into that knowledge?"

Noble's mind flashed back to another first step, thirteen years ago, when he'd had to tell his twenty-two-year-old daughter that her mother wasn't coming home.

Eleanor had died doing what she loved: photographing wild horses in Montana, trying to capture what she called "the space between moments."

Less than a year later, Sarah left for Seattle, unable to bear the weight of her grief and her father's determined blindness to the magic that had called to her mother. Eleanor had always been a free spirit, more like Sarah than him.

The camera they'd found had contained dozens of photos of empty meadows. Empty, at least, to everyone except Eleanor, who'd always insisted she could see what others missed. "The horses were there," Sarah had said at the funeral, her young face set with a certainty that frightened Noble. "Mom could see them. That's why she had to follow them."

After that, Noble delved even deeper into the structure and certainty of the hardware store. Sarah retreated into her mother's old journals and Rosa Martinez's stories.

Noble realized why Eleanor's camera had captured empty meadows. Some things cannot be captured or measured; they can only be experienced.

ANOTHER SOUND JOLTED him from his reverie as the door swung open.

She was here, finally. Sarah had come home. Noble hugged her silently as she cradled her father with the love she had missed desperately for the last twelve years. Jenny, too, hugged Sarah and realized what it would take to help Noble cross the threshold, if that were even possible.

The interior of Manning's Hardware had transformed in the dark. Everywhere, there was a sense of waiting, watching, and remembering. "Rosa knew this would happen," Jenny said softly, stepping into the strange space as if she had been expecting it all her life; perhaps she had. "She tried to prepare us, remember?"

Noble remembered he had found the old employee records several weeks earlier in a box he hadn't opened since his father's passing: Rosa Martinez, hired April 17, 1942.

"I never understood why my grandfather kept her on," he said, showing Sarah the yellowed document. "Business was struggling after the war started. Taking on a young widow with a baby made no practical sense."

Sarah ran her fingers over Rosa's signature. "Did you ever ask him?"

"Once. He said it was 'just until she found her feet.'" Noble smiled faintly. "Thirty years is a long time to find your feet."

"Jenny told me a different story," Sarah said. "About how Rosa walked into the store and went straight to that brass key on the wall, the one Mom gave me. According to Jenny, Rosa stopped mid-sentence while talking to your grandfather and said, "That key has been waiting."

Noble flipped through the yellowed pages, with all of Rosa's work hours carefully recorded. He remembered Rosa's sections of the store, where customers always found exactly what they needed, even when they didn't know what they were looking for.

"That's exactly how she put it. How did you know?"

Sarah reached into her pocket and pulled out the brass key, which seemed to catch light from angles where no light should fall. "Because she told me, Dad. The summer before

Mom died. While everyone thought I was helping stock shelves, Rosa taught me to listen."

Noble remembered, despite spending decades pushing those memories aside. Rosa Martinez, Jenny's grandmother, was Cedar Springs' unofficial spiritual guardian, the keeper of what she called "the old knowing."

She had worked in the store for thirty years, organizing tools by what she called their "intentions." Noble's father had tolerated it because Jenny always helped them find exactly what they needed, even if they didn't know what they were looking for.

"Your grandfather understood," Jenny said as if reading his thoughts. "He didn't believe in the old ways but respected them. That's why he gave Gran the key."

Noble stopped short. "What key?"

"The original key. The one Sarah has now. The one your mother gave her." Jenny touched a shelf, and ripples of light followed her fingers. "Gran said it was forged from the tools used to build this store. It holds the memory of every transaction, exchange, and moment when someone found exactly what they needed to build, repair, or create."

The shelves around them seemed to hum in response. Tools they'd sold decades ago appeared and disappeared like fish darting through the currents of deep ocean flows.

Noble saw hammers that his grandfather had used, saws that had constructed half the houses in Cedar Springs, and measuring tapes that had laid out gardens, nurseries, and graves.

"This isn't possible," he whispered, but his voice lacked

conviction. How often had he noticed things that didn't quite add up in the store?

Customers who found solutions to problems they hadn't even voiced. The way specific tools attracted the people who needed them.

"Gran used to say that Manning's Hardware is a magical place," Jenny continued, moving deeper into the transformed space. "They're where possibility lives, where broken things come to be made whole. Where dreams take physical form."

Noble thought of his beloved Eleanor, who constantly searched for magic in ordinary things. She loved the hardware store and would spend hours chatting with Rosa, while Noble focused on accounting and inventory.

After her tragic death, Rosa had tried to talk to him about Eleanor's "gift of seeing," but he'd shut down any conversation that ventured beyond the practical.

"Your Eleanor could see true," Rosa had told him once before her passing. "And Sarah has her eyes. The key knows this. It's been waiting."

It Was Beginning.

Now, watching illusory shadows dance across the walls of his utterly transformed store, Noble felt the weight of all he'd refused to see. The pressure of it made his chest tight and his vision narrow. This was too much. Too far beyond the ordered world he'd built so carefully.

Noble appeared to be in a walking trance, overwhelmed by all that had happened and yet afraid of what he now realized was his fate and purpose. For one evening, it was enough, maybe too much all at once. His head was spinning, and a sense of movement overtook him, yet he stood still.

Now, just really seeing it for the first time, he couldn't ignore it anymore. After all these years, something was about to change, and he could no longer deny the truth his eyes refused to hide, even though it could shatter the delicate balance of his mind.

Jenny sensed he was overwhelmed and watched as his feet tried to walk backward.

"Noble." Jenny's voice was gentle but firm. "Sarah needs you. The store needs you. The whole town needs what's awakening here."

But Noble was already turning away. The battle between his heart and mind was raging. The fight between destiny and history would soon be decided. One path leads him to his future, while the other keeps him frozen in the past, numb in the comfort of history.

His practical mind rebelled against what his soul was showing him. Tools don't cast living shadows. Spaces don't extend beyond their physical dimensions. Keys don't hold memories.

"All those years," Noble whispered, memories shifting like tectonic plates. "My father's insistence on precise organization, the careful cataloging of every transaction..."

"I'll come back in the morning," he said, his voice strange in his own ears. "When things are... normal again."

Jenny didn't try to stop him, but her voice followed him out.

"Some doors only open in the dark, Noble.
Some truths can only be seen in the spaces between what we
think we know."

He fled into the pre-dawn air and left the store, away from Jenny's knowing eyes and the weight of all he'd spent a lifetime not seeing. His phone buzzed in his pocket; Sarah called again, but he couldn't answer. Not now. Not until the world made sense again.

But as he drove home through streets that suddenly seemed full of shifting shadows and watching eyes, Noble remembered something else Rosa had once said:

> *"Running from magic doesn't make it less real.*
> *It just makes us less ready when it finally catches up."*

ARRIVING HOME after a short drive from the store, he reflected on all that had happened as reality began slowly returning. Noble gripped the steering wheel, his knuckles white against the leather. The numbers: There were always numbers to hold on to. Thirty-five years of inventory counts. Three generations of perfect ledgers. Thirty thousand transactions, all accounted for.

But now, each figure in his mind twisted into something else: Thirty-five years of ignored signs. Three generations of hidden truth. Thousands of moments when tools had intentions he pretended not to notice.

He almost missed the movement in his rearview mirror, a reflection shifting like a photograph developing in Eleanor's darkroom. For a moment, he saw his father's face overlaid on his own, wearing the same expression of controlled panic Noble remembered from certain evenings when the store had felt different.

"Structure," he whispered, his father's favorite word. But hadn't there been something else in his father's voice when he'd said it? Not just rigidity, but... reverence?

His phone buzzed again. It was Sarah. The screen flickered with her name, but behind the letters, he could have sworn he saw Eleanor's last photographs, those "empty" meadows that had never been empty.

His denial had created pressure points in reality, like fault lines in consciousness waiting for release. Each rationalization, tools that remembered their users, wood that whispered its history, and added to an energetic buildup that demanded a response.

Then, the Night Walker awakened from the darkness between moments; it was his time to intervene as he'd done many times over the decades, when the world was ready for the next step, as it was now. It wasn't chance but necessity… a calibrated reaction to Noble's resistance reaching critical mass.

"Measurement," he muttered, another of his father's mantras. "Everything can be measured." But even as he said it, he remembered the day Sarah, age seven, had asked why the hammers were singing. He'd sent her to help Jenny stock shelves instead of explaining that he heard it, too.

In that moment of truth, all he wanted was to be somewhere safe, just to ground himself and be reminded that he was still of sound mind.

Rushing inside and quickly moving to his home office, he pulled his father's old ledgers from the shelf of his perfect, ordered house, seeking comfort in their neat columns and precise calculations.

But for the first time, he noticed something else in the margins: tiny drawings, notes in his grandfather's hand about tools that "knew their work" and materials that "remembered their purpose." "*Wait a minute*... he looked again. *I could swear these notes weren't here before. I must be going crazy*... and for a moment, he felt the sweat bead on his brow and walked to the front door to get some air.

The sun was rising, painting the downtown below his wrap-around porch with crisp, even, measurable light. But Noble knew, with a terrified certainty, that nothing would ever look quite the same again. He reached for his phone and saw three missed calls from Sarah and two from Jenny.

He couldn't face either of them. Not yet. First, he needed to think, plan, and find some way to make sense of a world that suddenly refused to be measured.

But as he sat there, surrounded by the carefully maintained artifacts of his ordered life, Noble heard Rosa's voice one last time, a memory from long ago:

*"The choice isn't whether to believe in magic.
The choice is whether to face it standing up or running away.
But sooner or later, we all have to choose."*

4

THE SPACE BETWEEN

Noble rested and napped briefly on his father's La-Z-Boy, then awoke precisely at 6:15 a.m., as he had for thirty-five years. His body moved through familiar rhythms: the same oatmeal with measured teaspoons of brown sugar; the same blue shirt and khaki pants; the same route to Manning's Hardware in his meticulously maintained Volvo. Each habitual action laid another brick in the wall between last night's strangeness and today's comforting certainty. Everything seemed normal again. His carefully pressed but well-worn Dockers lay across the foot of the bed, his comfortable work boots waiting to step into a reality he recognized.

By the time he turned his key in the store's lock, the night's events had receded like tide marks on the sand, visible but increasingly faint. The brass key felt ordinary against his palm, just metal, not magic. The shadows cast by morning light behaved as shadows should. The tools hung in their designated places, silent and still, measurable and mundane.

The day's steady stream of customers anchored him further in comforting reality. Mrs. Peterson needed hinges for her

55

garden gate. The Wilsons were finishing their basement reno-
vation. Old Pete from the garage requested specialty screws
for a vintage car restoration. Noble filled each need with
practiced precision, each transaction reassuring that the world
remained firmly quantifiable.

Perhaps he believed he had been granted a reprieve while
updating the ledger that afternoon. Possibly, whatever responsibility had whispered through generations of Manning blood
would overlook him, seeking another keeper at another time.
The very thought released a tension he hadn't realized he had
been carrying on his shoulders, like putting down a weight he
had never acknowledged lifting.

THE DAY ENDED with all the usual activities: the last customer
picking up their cut lumber, the register balancing as always,
and the knowing smile of Jenny, who hadn't said a word
about the night before. She let Noble process all that had
happened and would wait patiently until it was time for the
unfolding to continue.

Like all who stand at the threshold of change, Noble needed
time to gather courage before certainty crumbled into the
unknown. For him, the unknown was where logic died, and
futures are too liquid to navigate.

Arriving home to an empty house, with a prepared meal
waiting to be warmed, he returned to his comfort zone.
Noble's study had always been his sanctuary, its mahogany
panels and leather-bound ledgers serving as a fortress against
uncertainty. Tonight, even these familiar walls seemed to
pulse with untold stories. The evening light caught his grandfather's old brass compass on the desk, and for a moment, he

thought he saw its needle spin wildly before settling in a direction it had never had before.

He tried his usual evening routine: checking the day's receipts, updating the perpetual inventory, and preparing tomorrow's orders. But each number refused to make sense. Yes, the math worked, but the numbers were wrong; he instinctively knew that. He checked a third time, and still the results were the same, but not "right," and he didn't know why.

The ledger's leather cover felt unusually warm beneath his fingers. He opened it and found his father's precise handwriting transforming before his eyes. Between the columns of figures, hidden messages emerged:

"Tools choosing their masters today" and "The shadows speak of change coming." His father's secret observations had been hidden in plain sight all these years.

A copper bell Eleanor had bought from a street vendor in Morocco, her last gift to him, chimed softly, though there was no breeze. Its tone carried memories of her voice:

"Everything's alive, Noble. Everything's connected. You must learn to see between the lines you love so much."

The grandfather clock struck 9:48 p.m. when the shadows in Noble's study began to move against the lamplight. The leather chair across from his desk creaked without being touched. The ledger pages ruffled, revealing his grandfather's hidden notes about tools that sang and materials that remembered. *Why hadn't I seen these before?* He thought as notes slowly materialized.

Three knocks echoed through the house, not on the door, but seemingly through the walls themselves as if the house's

bones were conducting sound from another reality. The
temperature dropped, and Noble caught the scent of ancient
wood, forge fire, and something wilder, like starlight distilled
into musk.

When he opened the door, darkness gathered into human
form. He stepped back, at first afraid, but soon realized that
he could do nothing but allow the night to unfold as it was.

The Night Walker emerged from these shadows like a photograph developing under the red glow of the darkroom safe-
light, his presence carrying the weight of every human
moment when safety gives way to possibility, when what
we've always known meets what we've always sensed.

His crinkled, weathered leather apron held indefinite depths
where tools shifted between forms. Now a hammer, now a
key, now something for which Noble had no name. Under his
wide-brimmed hat, his eyes reflected landscapes from times
that had never been and places that didn't exist on maps.

"Thomas Manning's son, grandson of the founder, keeper of
the third generation," the figure said, his voice carrying
echoes of iron on an anvil, trees growing through centuries,
and stories being born.

"The measurer. The one who tries to put borders around the
borderless."

He smiled, and in that expression, Noble saw every customer
who'd ever entered Manning's seeking one thing but needing
another.

"You've been expecting me, though you don't know it yet."

The Night Walker's eyes reflected landscapes Noble had
never seen, yet somehow recognized. "I am older than this
town, older than the cedar grove itself." His voice carried

echoes of ancient tools at work, of shadows lengthening across forgotten paths. "I walk between what is and what could be, appearing when places like Manning's Hardware stand at the edge of remembering their true purpose."

"Are there... others like you?" Noble asked, the question emerging from some deeper part of himself.

The Night Walker's smile held a mix of starlight and shadow. "Threshold guardians walk wherever worlds meet. We remember the old ways of crossing because someone must show others that the impossible is just the possible waiting to be believed."

He gestured at the window where Cedar Springs slept, unaware of its impending awakening. "This town has always been special, built at a convergence of realities. Manning's Hardware stands at its center, a crossroad that your family has maintained, even when they didn't understand what they were guarding."

Noble felt words forming in his throat: rational questions about identity and purpose, but deeper truths emerged. "You're what Eleanor could see, aren't you? What Sarah tried to tell me about? What Rosa always knew?"

His father's voice echoed in his memory:

"A Manning measures twice and believes once." But there had been moments, brief, quickly hidden, when he'd caught his father staring at tools that hummed with their light or tracing letters in Rosa's ledger with trembling fingers.

Once, he'd found his father in the lumber aisle at midnight, watching shadows dance between the boards. "Sometimes," he would hear his father whisper, not realizing Noble was there, "measuring isn't enough."

The Night Walker moved past Noble with liquid grace, each step leaving momentary impressions of other times and places.

The room's familiar dimensions shifted like a measuring tape stretched beyond its markings. Each breath carried traces of Eleanor's darkroom chemicals mingling with Rosa's healing teas, scents that had always been there, he realized, waiting for him to notice what his careful inventories had never counted.

"Your wife understood the language of in-between spaces," he said, settling into Noble's reading chair as if he'd emerged from it. "Eleanor could see past the surfaces of things to their singing hearts. It's why she chased those invisible horses. She knew some truths can only be captured by not trying to capture them at all."

"Your grandmother's dishes," he said, nodding at the cabinet Noble's mother had left him. The crystal glasses inside chimed softly, though there was no breeze. "It holds more stories than tea now. But then, most things do if we know how to listen."

The Night Walker's presence filled the room with memories Noble had spent decades suppressing. "How do you know about Eleanor?" he asked, though the answer resonated in his bones before the question left his lips.

"The same way I know about Rosa Martinez and her sight-gift. In the same way, I know about your grandfather Thomas and his secret writings. And, the same way, I know that your daughter Sarah holds a key that's older than this town."

The Night Walker leaned forward, and reality rippled around him. "The same way I know that you're standing at a sacred crossroad, Noble Manning, and everything depends on your chosen path."

"But I don't…" Noble stammered, trying to get the words out.

"Yes, you do." The man's voice was gentle but firm, resonating in Noble's bones.

"You've always believed… You've just spent your life building walls against that belief, measuring what can't be measured and trying to contain what was meant to flow."

He gestured at the ledgers on Noble's desk, and the numbers danced like fireflies before settling back into their neat columns. "Even now, you're seeking answers in numbers while magic runs through your blood like starlight reflections on water."

The room suddenly felt too small, and the air was thick with possibility. Noble stood up and walked closer. "The store…" he began.

"Is what it has always been: a crossroad, a doorway, a portal. A place where the visible and invisible worlds meet, and you've known it all along. You didn't have the guts to admit it because if you had, you'd have to do something about it, and you weren't about to change, were you?"

Noble was visibly repelled at that statement. "What am I supposed to do?"

"Just look at what's already in front of you. Surely, you cannot deny what you see." The Night Walker stood. His apron shifted, and tools glimpsed in its depths, their shapes changing in the candlelight.

"Every tool in the store is a key that unlocks transformation. just as every person has tools they haven't learned to use, gifts they've refused, truths they've avoided, and possibilities they've feared to step into. Manning's Hardware makes visible what exists in every soul, that sacred space where we choose between remaining what we were or becoming who we might be."

Noble's eyes shifted down, thinking of his own experience. "I can't do this alone, I don't know the way…"

"But you do." The Night Walker stepped closer now. "Rosa Martinez was a true keeper. She understood that some doors need more than physical keys." His eyes reflected possibilities Noble couldn't see in his imagination. "She came to Cedar Springs because the store called her, just as it called your grandfather before her, just as it's calling Sarah now."

"But why? Why now? Why us?"

"Because transitions aren't personal, Noble. They're universal. When enough people reach their own crossroads simultaneously, the very fabric of reality shifts, and the more dominant one, the right one, becomes true. Cedar Springs is at a crossroads now. Manning's Hardware has always been more than just a store; you have known that for years. It has served as a sanctuary for those in transition, a place where people find the tools they need and the courage to build something new."

The Night Walker turned away, his movement rippling through reality like stones dropped in still water. "The threshold guardians walk between what is and what could be. We remember the old ways of crossing because someone has to show others that the impossible is just the possible waiting to be believed."

Reality bent around him like light through Eleanor's camera lens, showing Noble glimpses of other Manning's Hardware stores, parallel versions with different choices. In one, he saw himself learning Rosa's wisdom instead of hiding behind inventory sheets. In another, he stood beside Eleanor as she photographed the invisible horses, finally seeing what she saw.

The Night Walker reached into his apron, leather creaking like an old door opening.

The walls around him held their breath as he withdrew a key gleaming with inner fire.

Unlike Sarah's key, this one carried marks Noble recognized from his grandfather's journal margins, symbols he'd dismissed as idle doodles but now recognized as a language older than words.

As Noble's fingers closed around it, the metal sang against his skin. Images cascaded through his mind: his grandfather and Rosa sharing a knowing look over inventory sheets that contained more than numbers; Eleanor in her darkroom, explaining how reality could bend around the truth; Sarah at age seven, arranging tools by their "songs" rather than their functions.

"I can see…" Noble whispered as his hand clutched the key. The warmth of the key opened a portal inside; he experienced what Eleanor had tried to convey: how emotions influenced certain tools, designating them for specific destinies. He suddenly understood Rosa's subtle magic, how she would guide troubled souls to exactly what they needed, whether they knew it or not.

"Tomorrow," the Night Walker said, his form beginning to blur like night mist catching dawn's rays, "each person who walks through that door carries two needs. The one they can name and the one they can't. A nail to hang a picture, yes, but also the courage to make a house feel like home again. A wrench to fix a leak, but also the strength to repair what's broken in their lives."

His form became more translucent as he turned to leave, but his voice grew stronger. "Sarah has appeared to you, no longer just as your daughter, but as someone who never needed to learn how to see magic. She never learned to stop seeing it, just like her mother, Rosa, and you, before you chose to forget. Yet, her struggle lay in trying to suppress it, and it seems the time has come for both of you to accept the truth and embrace your destiny."

"The truest crossroad isn't in your store, Noble Manning. It's in your heart. And tomorrow, you'll either step into the full power of who you are or spend the rest of your life wondering what might have been."

He moved toward the door with liquid grace, then paused, moonlight bent around him like water around stones. "You know the most challenging thing about crossroads moments, Noble?

They ask us to trust what we don't know how to believe,
To step forward when we can't see the path,
To become what we don't know how to be."

His translucent smile held starlight and shadow. "But here's the secret," the Night Walker continued.

"The path appears when you take the first step.
Not before. Never before."

The key pulsed in Noble's hand one final time, and he thought of Eleanor's beautiful visions and empty photographs. Had they been empty because she was photographing paths that could only be seen by walking them?

"The truest crossroads live in every heart that has ever faced the choice between comfortable blindness and costly sight. Tomorrow is that universal moment when you can no longer pretend not to see what you see, feel what you feel, and know what you undoubtedly know."

Then he was gone, though Noble couldn't remember seeing him leave. The moonlight through his study windows transformed ordinary shadows into doorways, and for the first time in decades, Noble didn't look away.

His phone buzzed. Jenny's message glowed: "The store's opening early today. Sarah's already there. Time to choose your path."

Noble stood inside the empty study, watching the space where the Night Walker had been. The key was warm against his palm as he walked out, standing there watching the whole town glow with a sense of wonder. *What will become of us?* he pondered, as he held his gaze steady.

The familiar streets of Cedar Springs unfolded below, but now he perceived them differently. Each house, garden, and garage held tales of transformation that began in his store.

Dawn painted the eastern sky exploding in colors that reminded him of Eleanor's last photographs. The key pulsed once, and Noble felt something shift inside him. Not a dramatic transformation, but a quiet remembering of who he'd always been beneath the careful numbers and precise measurements as he wondered for the first time in a long time, *Who am I really?*

Sarah waited at the store, holding her own key, feeling the becoming of this legacy; of seeing between moments. And for the first time since Eleanor's death, Noble felt ready to step into a world where not everything needed to be measured to be true.

It was time to walk a different path. It was time to become a different kind of pathfinder.

5

CROSSROADS

Noble stood before Manning's Hardware in the crystalline morning light, two keys warm against his palm: the familiar brass one he'd used for decades and the ancient one the Night Walker had given him, vibrating with a subtle resonance.

The store's windows reflected a glowing sky in ways that didn't quite match the sky behind him, as if they were showing dawn from another time.

Sarah's car was already in the lot, and a thin spiral of vapor rose from a coffee cup on its hood. The sight hit him with unexpected force; how many mornings had Eleanor's coffee sat in that same spot, steam rising like prayers to ascended souls?

The memory carried her darkroom scent, that mixture of chemistry and possibility that had always clung to her clothes.

Inside, he saw shadows moving that didn't match the bodies casting them. One looked almost like Rosa, arranging tools, showing Jenny what to look for.

67

Another could have been his grandfather, measuring more than just timber against his yardstick. The glass separating him from these possibly distant memories appeared to ripple like disturbed water.

"Dad…"

Sarah stood in the doorway, Eleanor's camera both shield and burden. She saw herself at seven, perched on her mother's shoulders in the darkroom, watching images emerge from seemingly blank paper.

See how the magic makes the truth appear? Eleanor would say, her fingers dancing in the chemical bath. *That's what your gift is, sweetheart. You see what's true, even what's seen, but not always real.* Those moments in the darkroom had been their sanctuary, where Eleanor could teach Sarah about their shared sight without Noble's disapproving frown.

Each return to Cedar Springs had been more challenging, watching her father measure miracles into inventory sheets while the store's magic ran in her blood, beckoning her forward.

The key she wore: Rosa's key, her grandmother's key, now her key, gleamed against her shirt with that same inner light he'd seen in the Night Walker's eyes, pulsing with the weight of denied inheritance.

Sarah's return wasn't just physical. She carried the weight of twelve years spent running from her inheritance, trying to build a life where magic couldn't find her. But like her mother, she'd learned that some gifts can't be denied, only delayed.

She appeared younger and older than her thirty-five years, as if time had become fluid around her.

"You see them too now, don't you?" she asked softly. "The other versions of the store. The paths that could be."

Before he could answer, Jenny emerged from behind Sarah, silver-streaked hair catching the morning light like threads of destiny. She carried Rosa's old ledger, its pages ruffling in the wind he couldn't feel.

"The whole town's shifting," Jenny said, her voice echoing her grandmother's accent. "Look."

Noble turned. Cedar Springs was waking up, but not quite how it usually did. The bakery's windows reflected bread made by hands that faded in and out of sight.

The old courthouse steps rippled with the footprints of generations. People walked everywhere with a slightly out-of-time quality as if multiple versions of themselves were trying to occupy the same space.

The Night Walker's key flared with recognition, acknowledging truths Eleanor had tried to show him through her lens.

Noble stepped toward the door, suddenly conscious of every movement, as if each step could take him in a different direction than intended. The keys in his palm seemed to pulse in alternating rhythms: the familiar one kept time with his heartbeat, and the ancient one beat to a deeper, older drum.

"Wait," Sarah said, reaching for his arm. Her touch triggered images flickering through his mind: Eleanor showing her how to focus a camera, Rosa teaching her to read the grain in wood, his mother watching her play with that brass key as a child.

"There's something you need to see first."

She lifted her mother's camera, its ancient leather strap creaking like whispered secrets spoken between words. Through its viewfinder, the storefront transformed. Layers of time became visible, like translucent pages in an infinite book.

Through the viewfinder, Noble saw what every person sees in moments of truth. Not just what is, but what could be if we dare to step beyond our carefully constructed walls, deeper to the core.

Noble saw the original wooden structure his grandfather had built, the addition his father had overseen, and the modern renovations he'd implemented himself. But he also saw versions that had never existed. Possibilities shimmered like heat waves on summer pavement.

She lowered the camera, her eyes holding that same endless depth the Night Walkers had.

"Mom could always see them," Sarah said, her voice catching. "I spent years trying not to. I pursued a career in museum conservation, a practical and measurable field. But every artifact I restored revealed its stories; every photograph I preserved showed layers of possibility. Like you, Dad, I tried to hide from who I am. Ultimately, Mom photographed what we could become if we stopped running from our gifts.

The store is like that now.
All possibilities are awakening at once.

"There's something else," Sarah said, reaching into her camera bag. She withdrew a small, weathered personal journal, its pages swollen with moisture and the passage of time. "I found this in Mom's old darkroom stuff last night. It was hidden behind the boxes."

The journal's cover bore Eleanor's distinctive swooping script: "What Light Cannot Capture." Noble's hands trembled as Sarah opened it to a marked page:

The store speaks louder each day. Tools rearrange themselves when no one's looking. Customer shadows tell stories their owners haven't lived yet. Noble tries so hard not to see, measuring miracles into inventory counts. But Sarah, my brilliant, seeing Sarah, she notices everything. Today, she asked why the hammers were singing.

I now understand why some choose blindness. Seeing too much is like staring at the sun. Reality fractures into infinite possibilities. Which path is true? Which future should we create? The crossroads multiply until every step feels like a universe-shifting choice.

Rosa warns me about chasing visions too far. "Some truths aren't meant to be captured," she says, "only witnessed." But how can I stop looking when each photograph shows another layer of what could be?

The store is evolving. The whole town is.

Those who can see must choose to become channels for transformation or break under its weight. I see Sarah watching me, learning to hide her gift from her father. My heart breaks, knowing she'll face this choice, too.

Noble will understand one day. The Manning blood carries more than just merchant sense. But timing matters. Rosa says that every soul must find its own crossroads. Force the moment too soon, and the sight becomes blinding rather than illuminating.

The next entry was dated three days before Eleanor's final trip:

The wild horses are calling, the ones that run between worlds. They show me doorways, but I can't tell if I'm meant to photograph or follow them. Sarah sees them, too, though she pretends not to. She'll be safer that way until it's time.

Noble, if you read this, forgive yourself for choosing safety. Sometimes, we need darkness to let our eyes adjust to light. But the store is stirring now. Change is coming, ready or not. When it does, remember that transformation is about finally being what we've always been and are meant to be.

Sarah, my seeing girl: Your gift is not a curse. It's a bridge between what is and what could be. Learn from my mistakes: don't chase the visions. Let them come to you. And when the store calls, remember that some doors need two keys to open: your father's grounding and your sight combined.

Noble looked up from the pages, meeting Sarah's tear-bright eyes. The keys in his palm pulsed with Eleanor's last truth: transformation required vision and foundation, magic and measure, seeing and being seen.

Sarah held the journal while Nobel read it. His trembling hands, the tears streaming down his face, all of it was too much all at once, yet he was now ready to see those words, to feel those feelings, and reconnect with his beloved Eleanor in a way he finally could see her, when for all those years he wished he could.

They hugged and sobbed as their collective pain merged in love, and pride rose to replace it like a cleansing rain after a dusty day. Noble and Sarah uncovered what was hidden and, united in spirit as a family, fulfilled their destiny.

"Dad," Sarah called. "There's one more thing I want to show you. Come with me."

Sarah led him down into Eleanor's old darkroom, which had been dismantled long ago. Only boxes and a few dusty filing cabinets remained.

He hadn't entered this basement space since her death, leaving it untouched like a shrine, afraid of what he might have to confront. The familiar scent of developing chemicals still lingered, though no photographs had been processed here in years.

Sarah, holding the ancient camera, its shutter clicking by itself all afternoon, capturing images of things between moments.

"Open the bottom drawer," she said.

Reluctantly, he opened her old filing cabinet. Inside, there were hundreds of prints labeled in her flowing script: "Between Moments: Spring 1998," "Threshold Crossings: Summer 2001," and "The Horses: Final Series."

Noble picked up the last folder, remembering how he'd dismissed these photos as empty meadows. But now, with his transformed vision, he saw what Eleanor had been trying to show him: shapes moving between possibilities, doorways opening between worlds, magic that had always existed if he'd only been brave enough to see it.

"I was so afraid," he whispered to the quiet room. "… of what accepting it would mean."

He discovered her final journal beneath the prints, its pages still adorned with her favorite photos. Her words pierced him like hooks in his heart:

Noble sees it too, though he pretends not otherwise. Each time the tools sing, or the shadows dance, I watch him choose blindness over sight. What terrifies him is the responsibility that comes with seeing truly. The same weight his father carried that his grandfather bore before him. The Manning gift is keeping a doorway open between worlds. But doors can be closed as well as opened, and Noble fears the price of holding them wide.

The keys at his chest hummed as he read, resonating with Eleanor's understanding. He'd always thought she chased magic because she couldn't accept reality. Now he understood. She'd seen reality more clearly than anyone, including the price it demanded.

Another entry, dated just days before her final trip:

The horses are running again, carrying possibilities between worlds. They're gathering, preparing for something. Sarah sees them, too, though she's learning to hide it, just like her father does. But hiding from magic doesn't make it less real; it simply makes us less ready when it finally catches up.

Noble will face his moment soon. I've seen it in the shadows between moments, in how the store's tools have started singing louder. He'll have to choose between the safety of blindness and the cost of truly seeing. I pray he remembers what his father didn't dare to see, that some prices are worth paying, some transformations worth their pain.

Just three days before her tragic accident, Eleanor had a vivid dream about the horses in Montana's Glacier National Park. Over the last several months, she'd curated a series of images taken locally, around Cedar Springs. Then, when a picture emerged in the chemical bath: wild horses running across terrain she'd never photographed, their forms translucent against a landscape that existed between dimensions, she realized something was shifting. Quickly.

She packed her camera gear that night, leaving Noble a note about photographing wildlife for a magazine assignment. The lie came easily. How could she explain that her photographs were calling her toward something she couldn't name?

The horses appeared on her second day in the park. Eleanor was photographing an empty meadow when her viewfinder filled with movement: a herd of mustangs that existed only between the frames of ordinary sight. Through her lens, they were solid as stone. When she lowered the camera, the meadow stood vacant.

She followed them for three days, her film capturing what her eyes couldn't hold. The horses led her deeper into the wilderness, away from marked trails and ranger stations. Each photograph revealed more of their nature: they were thresholds themselves. Were they horses or were they pathways leading to something she needed to see, to experience?

On the fourth morning, Eleanor woke to find a single horse standing at the edge of her camp. Through her camera lens, she could see this magnificent creature: a coat that held starlight, a mane that flowed like liquid time, and eyes that reflected landscapes from worlds that had never been. The mare stepped forward, and Eleanor understood.

He was inviting her to follow him home.

Eleanor packed her camera carefully, hands trembling with recognition of the choice before her. She could return to Cedar Springs, to Noble's determined blindness and Sarah's growing gift. She could spend her remaining years trying to show others what they refused to see, documenting magic for eyes that preferred surfaces.

Or she could step into the space between moments and never return.

The horse began moving as dawn painted the sky in colors that didn't exist on any palette. Eleanor followed, her camera clicking constantly, as she tried to capture the sensation of walking between worlds. The meadow grass beneath her feet felt both solid and ethereal. The air tasted of copper and futures.

Her final photograph showed the moment of transition: Eleanor's own shadow stretching toward another dimension while her body remained tethered to the physical world. The horse, having joined his herd, waited just beyond reach, patiently, as teachers who understood the difficulty of the lesson.

Eleanor chose to go forward. She stepped fully into the space between moments, her camera slipped from her physical fingers, capturing one last image: an empty meadow that had never been empty, holding the echo of a woman who loved truth more than safety, wonder more than wisdom.

Rangers found her camera two days later. The film inside contained dozens of images of vacant landscapes, each frame perfectly exposed, technically flawless, emotionally devastating in its emptiness. They never found Eleanor's body. She had become part of the spaces she'd spent her life photographing, existing now in the realm between what ordinary cameras capture and what eyes can see, in the hands of very special photographers.

Noble received the developed photographs and the camera in its case three weeks later. He saw empty meadows and called them Eleanor's final artistic statement. He never noticed how the grass bent in patterns that suggested recent passage, how the light fell in ways that implied presence just beyond the frame's edge.

Sarah looked at the same images and saw her inheritance: the gift of seeing between worlds, the responsibility of choosing when to follow visions and when to remain grounded. Eleanor's photographs became both a legacy and a warning, showing the beauty of sight and the cost of sight without a foundation.

JENNY OPENED ROSA'S LEDGER, its pages rustling with that same otherworldly breeze. "Gran wrote about this. About times when the boundaries between what is and what could be grow thin, about this very moment when all is finally visible.

"When places remember their true purpose." Her finger traced lines of her grandmother's flowing script. "She called them crossroads, moments when change becomes not just possible but necessary."

Jenny moved between realities with the ease of someone who'd never learned to doubt magic, who'd grown up under-standing that every tool could build two things: what the customer asked for and what their soul needed.

Noble felt the weight of both keys in his hand, the familiar and the mysterious, the measured and the infinite. The door before him seemed to multiply, showing different versions of itself, different thresholds to cross.

"Which one is real?" he whispered.

"They all are," Jenny said, her voice echoing Rosa's wisdom. "That's what Gran tried to tell us.

Reality is more than a single path - it's all the paths at once, until we choose which one to walk."

Sarah raised the camera again, its shutter clicking with a sound like certainty finding imagination.

"Look, Dad. Look..."

Through the viewfinder, Noble saw his customers, finally, as they could be. In her garden, Mrs. Chen guided the little hands of her grandchildren to plant seedlings and showed them the way.

Bill Baxter was building a front porch and a new foundation for his life. The hardware store wasn't just selling tools; it offered possibilities, chances, and transformations.

The key the Night Walker had given him grew almost hot against his palm. The air around them thickened with potential, with change, with choice.

"I don't know how to take the next step..." Noble started, but Sarah shook her head.

"Yes, you do. You always have. That's why the store chose our family and called Rosa. Why Mom could see what others couldn't." She touched the key at her throat. "We're not just keepers of hardware, Dad. We're keepers of crossroads, protectors of possibilities, in the lives of those around us.

Jenny stepped forward, holding her grandmother's ledger like a map to unknown territories.

Every transition begins with a single step.
Every transformation begins with a single moment of trust.

Noble looked down at the keys in his hand, then up at the multiple versions of the door before him. In each reflection, he saw a different version of himself: the practical businessman his father had trained, the curious boy who'd listened to Rosa's stories, the husband who'd loved Eleanor deeply without understanding the magic, the father who'd tried to protect Sarah from truths he had been afraid to face.

The morning light shifted, catching the brass of both keys, old and new, known and mysterious. Their combined warmth spread through his arm and chest into places long closed to possibility.

Noble raised both keys, their metal singing against each other like tuning forks resonating in harmony. The door before him shifted and changed, showing all its possible versions and potential thresholds. But one in particular felt right, the one that lit up for him.

Instead of confusion, he felt something else: a clarity that reminded him of Eleanor's smile, Rosa's knowing eyes, and Sarah's unfailing sight.

You don't choose the door, he whispered, understanding flowing like spring water. *You choose who you become when you walk through it.*

Sarah clicked the shutter release, capturing the moment his father's practical training and Rosa's ancient wisdom finally merged.

Jenny's grandmother's ledger fluttered open to a page he'd never seen. Rosa's handwriting spoke of moments when the keeper became the key.

Noble stepped forward. Both keys turned in locks that existed in multiple realities at once. The scent that washed over him carried wood shavings, potential futures, metal filings, and transformation, paint thinners, and wonder.

"We need to understand what's happening to the whole town,"

Sarah said, her camera hanging ready. "The store isn't changing in isolation."

Noble nodded, feeling both keys pulse against his chest in agreement. "The Night Walker said something about crossroads... not just our store, but the entire town."

The three of them stepped out into Cedar Springs' morning air. The familiar streets Noble had walked for decades now seemed alive with new possibilities. As they moved past Mrs. Chen's bakery, the scent of her bread carried more than just yeast and flour; it held memories of distant homelands and futures not yet baked.

"Look," Jenny whispered, pointing to the old courthouse square where the town's cedar trees stood sentinel. Their ancient branches swayed in patterns that had nothing to do with wind, casting shadows that told stories of the land before the town existed.

Noble watched as ordinary townspeople went about their day, some oblivious to the changes, while others paused with expressions of wonder or confusion as reality rippled around them. "They're starting to feel it too," he said.

"This is why we're here," Sarah said firmly, her voice carrying Eleanor's certainty. "To witness the awakening, and to guide it. To help Cedar Springs remember what it was always meant to be, a place where the ordinary and extraordinary could safely meet."

Jenny nodded, Rosa's ledger clutched to her chest. "Gran wrote about this. About how Manning's Hardware was just the first threshold. The anchor point for something larger."

Standing in the town square, watching Cedar Springs begin to shimmer between what it had always appeared to be and what it truly was, Noble finally understood their purpose.

"We're guardians of a crossroads between worlds. And our task isn't just to accept the magic... It's to help everyone else find their way through the transformation," he said as the two keys gently hummed in sync. Sarah finished. "To show them how to balance wonder and wisdom, just as you're learning to do."

As they walked back toward Manning's Hardware, Noble felt a new resolve. This would be more about embracing the store's awakening and guiding an entire community through a sacred threshold. The actual work was just beginning.

The inside of Manning's Hardware had become a series of infinite pathways, all leading to probabilities, all of which were true.

Tools lined shelves that stretched into seemingly infinite spaces; their dimensions shifted, telling stories of everything they had built or could build. The old register chimed with transactions from the past and future. The seed bins glowed, revealing glimpses of gardens not yet planted. The lumber inventory sang of homes not yet built, lives not yet lived, families to be.

"Oh," Sarah breathed, her camera capturing impossibilities. "This is what Mom was trying to show us."

Jenny moved past them both, her fingers trailing along shelf edges that rippled like water at her touch.

Rosa's ledger tucked under her arm. The awakening store responded to her presence differently than to Noble's or Sarah's. Where they experienced wonder tinged with uncertainty, Jenny felt a sense of homecoming.

She had spent years maintaining the delicate balance Rosa
established: arranging inventory by both practical categories
and hidden relationships, guiding customers to purchases that
served needs they hadn't voiced, keeping the magic functional
rather than overwhelming. Now the store was remembering
its true nature, and Jenny's role was shifting from preserva-
tion to acceleration.

The sight gift flowed through her fingers as she touched
shelves and adjusted displays. Tools hummed with recognition under her hands. Wood grain revealed its preferred
arrangements. Even the dust motes seemed to dance in
patterns that enhanced the store's awakening energy.

She opened Rosa's ledger to a page that had appeared blank
the previous day. Now words flowed across it in her grandmother's script:

*When the keeper becomes ready, the gift expands beyond
arrangement into activation.*

Jenny's struggle taught her to ground visions in practical
systems. Now she teaches the store to do the same.

Jenny felt the truth of those words as she worked. Each
adjustment she made not only organized the physical space
but also strengthened the magical infrastructure. She was
creating sustainable pathways for wonder to flow through
commerce, building frameworks that would allow the awakening to continue without overwhelming customers or bank-
rupting the business.

Mrs. Chen entered with her basket of transformed bread,
followed by Jack Thompson carrying wood that gleamed with
inner light. They moved naturally toward the sections Jenny
had just rearranged, finding exactly what they needed, as
always.

"How do you know where everything should go?" Mrs. Chen asked, watching Jenny guide her toward specialized baking supplies she hadn't known the store carried.

"My grandmother taught me to listen," Jenny replied, her fingers trailing along shelves that reorganized themselves subtly in her wake. "Every tool wants to find its proper work. Every customer has hidden needs they haven't named. My job is to help them meet each other."

She felt Rosa's approval in the way the morning light caught the floating dust particles, in how the old register chimed with deeper harmonies, in the subtle shift of the store's energy toward sustainable transformation rather than chaotic awakening.

This was her true inheritance: not just the ability to see hidden patterns, but the strength to build foundations that would let magic flourish in the practical world. Rosa had planted the seeds. Jenny was teaching them to grow roots deep enough to weather any storm.

"Gran used to say that true hardware stores are where people come to build their dreams, with tools and with courage. With hope and trust in the unknown." Her voice carried echoes of Rosa's accent.

THE MORNING LIGHT streamed through the windows from different directions, as if from multiple suns, casting shifting shadows.

Each shadow held memories or possibilities: Rosa's organized tools now made sense to Noble. Looking through the eyes of understanding, Eleanor photographed the spaces between moments. He saw something new, and his grandfather, in secret, measured more than just lumber against his yardstick.

Noble felt the change moving through him like sap rising in spring. All his careful measurements, precise inventories, and need for control didn't disappear but transformed.

Numbers became stories. Inventory became possibilities. Control became stewardship.

"The store was always like this," he realized, watching past and future dance in the dust balls. "We just forgot how to see it."

A clock chimed somewhere; maybe it was the keys in his hand, Sarah's camera shutter, or the pages of Rosa's ledger turning in that etheric breeze.

Sounds rippled out through Cedar Springs like gentle waves approaching land. Through the windows, Noble could see the town responding. The bakery's bread awakened memories not yet made.

The courthouse steps rang with footsteps from many times at once. The park's trees cast shadows that grew dreams instead of darkness.

"It's starting," Sarah said, her voice thick with wonder. "The whole town is remembering what it could be."

Jenny opened Rosa's ledger wider, its pages showing the past and possible futures.

"When one crossroad awakens, others follow. Gran wrote about this: When changing itself changes when transformation becomes not just possible but necessary."

Noble felt the truth in his bones and blood, in the keys that had become warm as sunrise in his palm. Manning's Hardware had always been a threshold where the practical and the possible met and merged.

And he had always been more than just its keeper.

The first customers will be arriving soon. They would come seeking hardware, but now he knew what they were really looking for.

Soon, others would see the changes too, their eyes opening to possibilities like flowers to the sun. Others would take longer, seeing only what they expected to see, until the moment their own crossroads arrived.

Noble thought of the Night Walker's words:

The path only appears when you take the first step.

Now, standing in this transformed space with Sarah's camera clicking, Jenny's ledger whispering, and both keys humming with ancient magic in his hand, he understood.

The path now appeared because he'd finally become someone who could walk over that threshold, through that door, not knowing what he would find. Instead, he mustered the courage to discover who he would be if he did.

He turned to Sarah and Jenny, seeing them clearly for perhaps the first time, not just as his daughter and his employee but as fellow travelers, keepers of crossroads, and guides for others who would come seeking their own transformations.

"Well," he said, his voice echoing with all his selves, both past and possible, "shall we open the store?"

Sarah's smile held Eleanor's light. Jenny's nod carried Rosa's wisdom.

And somewhere, in the spaces between what was and what could be, Noble felt the Night Walker's approval like moonbeams from heaven.

The dawn had fully broken, and Cedar Springs was painted in colors he hadn't seen before this morning. People would be arriving soon.

The store had been patient, waiting while she found her way back. Unlike Eleanor, who'd chased magic until it consumed her, Sarah had learned to bridge worlds: to see possibility without losing sight of the present.

Now, Manning's Hardware needed Noble's grounding and Sarah's vision, practical tools, transformative power, measure, and magic... merged.

Now, as a guide, the key itself showed the way, now that Sarah had awakened to its mission. As it warmed against her skin, she felt its approval of this balance, this new way forward.

It was time to begin.

6

SHADOWS AND LIGHT

At precisely 8:17 a.m., Marcus Whitman from the bank pushed through the door with his battered briefcase and usual frown. He brought with him the sharp scent of starched cotton and rigid expectations.

The store's newly awakened magic seemed to recoil at his entrance.

"Manning," Marcus said, nodding, his voice carrying the weight of thirty years on the bank's board. "Got your quarterly figures here. Some concerns we need to discuss."

Noble felt both keys pulse against his chest. The keys hung on a leather cord Jenny had found on Rosa's old desk. The familiar key whispered of spreadsheets and profit margins while the ancient one hummed with more profound truths. The air between him and Marcus seemed to thicken with opposing realities.

Sarah held her camera as the shutter clicked automatically. Through its viewfinder, Noble knew Marcus would appear surrounded by chains of his own making, golden handcuffs of

87

spreadsheets and projections that had slowly squeezed the wonder from his world.

"Beautiful morning for possibilities, isn't it?" Noble heard himself say, the words carrying echoes of Rosa's accent, of Eleanor's laugh.

Marcus blinked, his frown deepening.

"Possibilities don't pay loans, Manning. These figures..."

He broke off, staring at the ledger he'd just opened, trying to ignore what was happening right in front of his eyes. Noble saw what had caught his attention. Stories were writing themselves in Rosa's flowing script between the columns of numbers.

Tales of first homes built with Manning hardware, gardens grown from seeds of hope, broken things… and people made whole.

"What kind of trick..." Marcus's voice faltered as the numbers on his pages shifted, revealing human worth instead of the financial stats he expected. Each transaction now carries its actual cost and reward measured in dreams restored, courage found, and possibilities awakened, not just dollars.

"I heard the rumors around town that Manning's Hardware is not the same as it used to be, and that's disturbing. Did you see the article in the *Times* yesterday?"

Noble felt the light dimming inside Marcus as he let fear override his senses. "No, I don't read newspapers much these days."

"There was an article about a consultant who restores towns to normal when they slip into this... what would you call it?

Fantasy? Maybe he should take a look at Manning's." Marcus mumbled that last part as he reflected on how numbers in his journal started shifting.

Behind the counter, Jenny opened Rosa's ledger, its pages rustling with that ethereal breeze. "Would you like to see what these numbers really mean, Mr. Whitman?"

The bank manager took an instinctive step backward, but Noble recognized the look in his eyes, the same one he'd seen in his own reflection just hours ago when certainty first began to crack and let the light in.

He walked toward him slowly as he watched the confusion take hold of Marcus, thinking he was here to discuss numbers, not hope and dreams.

"Marcus," Noble said gently, "when was the last time you built something with your own hands?"

Marcus became annoyed. "Noble, we have a real problem here, and all you want to do is talk about... this?" He pointed to the strange light from his journal, as numbers began floating about the surface.

Noble remained quiet, watching Marcus's struggle with what he was seeing in his ledger.

"Marcus? Have you ever built anything with your own two hands?" he asked again.

The question echoed in the transformed space. Marcus's grip tightened on his ledger as unwanted memories surfaced. The treehouse he had built for his son, now grown and gone to a city where nothing was made by hand. The garden box for his mother's roses was assembled with tools from Manning's Hardware. That was the last thing he'd made before spread-sheets replaced hammers and nails.

For a moment, Marcus felt something stir, a longing he'd buried under years of quarterly reports. A hammer on the wall seemed to catch his eye, and he found himself taking a half-step toward it before stopping abruptly.

"No." He snapped the ledger shut, the numbers returning to their standard black-and-white. "Noble, whatever this is, it's not sustainable. I've seen businesses chase fantasies before." His voice carried the authority of three decades in banking, but underneath lay something that might have been regret. "If this doesn't stop, you won't be able to stay profitable, and I don't have to tell you what happens next."

He straightened his tie, rebuilding his professional composure like armor. "The bank needs predictability, Noble. Numbers that add up. Reality that stays put." But his eyes lingered on the hammer for just a moment too long.

Noble smiled reassuringly. "After three generations of Mannings, do you think I would let that happen? You know who I am, and none of that is true. Now, what do you really want?"

Something was happening, shifting. Marcus was scared by what he felt. With a life of banking behind him, it was the only surety he had, the way of life he followed, and the path he chose. Yet in that moment, the pictures flooded his mind, the memories of starting with a young family, making furniture for the house, window boxes for his wife, toys for his little boy. A smile, a tear, a melting heart, something changed.

"I..." Marcus swallowed hard. "Tommy's kids are visiting next month. He mentioned maybe building them a playhouse..."

Noble nodded quietly, letting the words hang in the air between them.

Sarah's camera clicked, capturing the instant Marcus's armor of certainty cracked just slightly. Jenny moved quietly through the store; Rosa's ledger was tucked under her arm like a map to hidden treasure.

But the door chimed again before Marcus could explore what that crack might mean.

Harold Whitaker, president of the Cedar Springs Business Association, strode in, bringing the sharp scent of progress and impatience. The tools' shadows shortened farther, retreating from his practical stance and measuring eyes.

"Noble! Glad to catch you. We need to discuss these rumors about Manning's." Harold's voice carried the weight of commerce without wonder. "People are saying strange things. Confusion about prices, inventory that seems to change, odd lights in the windows after hours."

Noble felt the keys at his chest respond differently to Harold's presence: the familiar one warming with recognition, the ancient one growing cool with warning. Here was his first real test, a man who saw the world only in terms of profit and loss, who had spent decades paving over magic with modernization.

"What people are saying," Harold continued, pulling out his tablet with its gleaming screen, "is that Manning's isn't operating... normally. We adhere to the standards set by the business association. Expectations. We can't have member stores going..."

He waved his hand vaguely at the shelves where reality rippled like heat waves. "You know, this isn't normal. There are other towns where this kind of thing happened, and it wasn't a pretty picture. We need to get a hold of this nonsense before it runs out of control..." Harold mentioned that as he searched his bag for the *Times*, he had read about a consultant who had previously dealt with this problem.

Sarah stepped forward, Eleanor's camera hanging at her throat like a talisman and a guide… who can see what it was really showing.

"Would you like to see what normal really looks like, Mr. Whitaker?"

Before Harold could object, she pressed the viewfinder to his eye. Noble observed the moment of impact. Harold's complexion drained as he gazed at the actual Cedar Springs layered over the version he had tried to create.

The family-run shops were demolished, and modern cookie-cutter storefronts lined the streets. The dreams paved over by parking lots: the life force and potential discoveries sealed behind regulations and standardizations.

"Impossible," Harold whispered, but his voice lacked conviction. "This isn't... we can't..."

"Can't what?" Jenny's voice carried Rosa's accent more strongly now. "Can't remember what Cedar Springs was meant to be? What it could still become?"

She opened her grandmother's ledger, and Harold stumbled back as stories rose from its pages like tiny tornadoes spinning in harmony. Tales of the town's founding, shops that offered more than merchandise, and a community built on relationships as much as on dollars.

The air in the store became thick with possibility. He could now envision families in backyards cherishing time together, playing with toys that inspired futures and new relationships that, if nurtured, might last a lifetime.

But Harold's face hardened, his jaw tightening into lines of defiance. "This ends now, Manning. We'll hold an emergency board meeting as soon as possible. This... whatever it is... isn't good for business."

The threat hung like smoke in a candle-lit room, but Noble felt no fear. The keys at his chest hummed with ancient certainty. He understood now.

Every threshold crossed would bring both allies and adversaries. Every transformation would face those who fought to maintain the comfortable darkness of the familiar.

Still holding his ledger of transformed numbers, Marcus looked between Harold and Noble like a man witnessing the beginning of a storm.

The hammer on the wall gleamed brighter, and for a moment, Marcus felt the pull; hands that remembered how to build, a heart that remembered how to dream.

"I..." Marcus started, his voice uncertain. The ledger trembled in his grip as the numbers flickered between stories and statistics. "Tommy's kids are visiting next month. Maybe I should..."

He took a half-step toward Jenny, then stopped abruptly, professional training reasserting itself. "No. This is exactly what I'm talking about." He clutched the ledger tighter, forcing the numbers back to black and white. "Noble, I can't let personal sentiment cloud financial judgment."

Harold's face showed relief. "Exactly right, Marcus. Business is business."

But Marcus's eyes lingered on the lumber aisle, conflict written across his features. "The quarterly figures still need review," he said, though his voice lacked conviction. "Some things... some things have to come first."

Sarah's camera caught the moment when his shadow seemed to stretch in two directions at once, toward spreadsheets and toward possibility.

The door chimed again, a sound now filled with notes of possibility in its familiar ring. Mrs. Chen entered, bringing the aroma of fresh-baked bread and morning glory flowers.

Noble had always known she opened her bakery at dawn, but today he saw more: how her kneading of dough was a kind of magic, how her loaves carried memories of homes left behind and dreams still rising.

Each morning, Mrs. Chen's first loaves tasted of a new dawn and possibility. By noon, her sourdough had fermented time itself, each bite releasing an unseen opportunity and unrealized dreams. But customers really came for her sunset bread, the crusty boules that, when broken open, expanded into all possibilities, all at once.

Jack Thompson followed. His weathered hands were trailing wood shavings that curled like time's passage. Each spiral of pine carried whispers of the forest it once knew, while the oak dust in his hair hummed with decades of bird songs stored in its rings.

Then, Maria Rodriguez from the flower shop, her apron stained with colors that seemed to move like living things, trailed rivers of nearly invisible blooms from her shop. Her apron held the energy of a living garden: violet shadows that deepened like dusk, yellows spread like dawn breaking, and greens spiraled with the memory of growth. Some colors existed only between heartbeats, while others whispered stories of seeds dreaming beneath winter soil.

The roses tucked in her pocket had learned to bloom in shades of courage, while the daisy chain around her wrist wove fragments of joy into a living bracelet.

One by one, the old heart of Cedar Springs arrived, each bringing their own awakening magic, remembering at last how to answer a call their souls had always whispered.

Harold's tablet screen flickered faster, numbers fighting with stories for dominance.

"This isn't a town meeting," he snapped, but uncertainty had crept into his voice.

"Isn't it?" Mrs. Chen's accent echoed Rosa's wisdom. "Strange things have been happening all morning. My bread speaks of homes across oceans. Jack's wood whispers of forests. Maria's flowers bloom with memories." She smiled at Noble. "Finally, the hardware store remembers, too."

The keys at Noble's chest hummed with recognition. These customers... They are keepers of their own kinds of magic, hidden beneath commerce, waiting for permission to emerge.

"You're all crazy!" Harold said, but his grip on the tablet had whitened his knuckles. "This town needs progress, not... fantasy."

"Progress?" Jack's quiet voice carried the strength of well-seasoned wood. "Like tearing down the old theater for a parking lot? Like replacing Miller's Books with a chain store?"

Sarah's camera clicked, and Noble knew she was capturing all the moments Cedar Springs had chosen: commerce over community, efficiency over magic.

"The business association exists to protect..." Harold began, but Maria interrupted him.

"To protect what? The same plans that shut down my mother's restaurant? That paved over the community garden for office space?" Her flowers seemed to glow with defiance. "Maybe it's time for a different kind of protection!"

Jenny had returned with Marcus, who now held a piece of pine in his hands like a newly discovered future. Rosa's ledger lay open on the counter between them, its pages turning in the invisible breeze. It showed the true history of Cedar Springs, in dreams and possibilities.

"A town isn't spreadsheets, Harold." Noble felt the words rise from somewhere deeper than memory.

"It's stories. It's magic. It's people and their gifts. It's a transformation. It's who we are!"

"It's business," Harold countered, but the tablet in his hands had gone dark, its screen reflecting only shadows of what could be.

"It's both," Noble said, understanding flowing through him like spring water. "That's what Manning's has always been, a place where dreams meet possibilities, where hammers build both houses and hopes. Where nails fasten intention as firmly as wood."

The store seemed to pulse with approval. Shadows that danced with purpose. The old register chimed a harmony of commerce and wonder. Even the dust flicks sparked with possibilities.

Harold didn't seem convinced. The fear of change seeped through his skin as he gripped his tablet even tighter than before. "The emergency board meeting stands," Harold said, backing toward the door. "This ends today."

But Noble saw what Harold couldn't, how the town was already changing. Through the windows, Cedar Springs shimmered with awakening magic. Mrs. Chen's bread. Jack's sawdust. Maria's flowers. All telling stories of possibility.

And others were coming. Through Sarah's camera lens, Noble could see local community members, people drawn to the awakening, carrying their own magic disguised as ordinary life.

The high school art teacher whose paintings captured the imagination more than light, the librarian who knew books held more than words, and the car mechanic who intuitively sensed problems in people as well as engines.

"Let him call his meeting," Mrs. Chen said after Harold had gone, her voice rich with wisdom and determination. "Some things can't be voted away. Some magic, once remembered, refuses to be forgotten."

There was a rustling sound as Marcus held a pristine pine plank, glowing with the memories of an old-growth forest filled with a century of stories.

He ran his hands along the pine board, feeling the history in its grain. "I'll need more than lumber for this playhouse," he said softly. "I'll need..."

"Permission?" Jenny smiled Rosa's smile and continued. "To build something real? To remember who you were before spreadsheets?"

"To remember who we all were," Jack added, his calloused hands touching tools that hummed with recognition. "Before, progress meant forgetting dreams, not anymore!"

Noble felt the truth in both keys. The real Manning's Hardware had always been a crossing point and, yes, also a gathering place.

A sanctuary for those who needed both tools and transformation.

"Maybe another time", he said as he pushed aside his true desires, instead doing the right thing.

The morning light streamed through windows that displayed multiple versions of Cedar Springs: what was, what could be, and what was beginning to become.

The battle lines were drawn between competing realities: Harold's world of pure commerce or one where magic and practicality danced together like light and shadow.

Noble touched both keys, feeling their pulse like twin hearts against his chest. The confrontation had revealed the battle lines, but nothing was settled. Every face in the store told a different story.

Sarah stood with her camera ready, and Jenny clutched Rosa's ledger like a shield. Mrs. Chen, Jack, and Maria had clearly chosen their side. But Marcus lingered near the door, his ledger closed, his expression unreadable. Harold had stormed out without another word, his threats hanging in the air like smoke.

"This won't end here," Jenny said quietly, watching Marcus through the window as he sat in his car, making no move to leave. "Look at him. He wants to believe, but fear keeps pulling him back."

Noble followed her gaze. Marcus held his phone, finger hovering over the screen, and made calls. To whom?

"Harold will fight this," Sarah said, her camera capturing the shadows lengthening across the store. "He won't accept what happened tonight."

Through the window, they watched Harold's car pull up beside Marcus. The two men spoke through their windows, their conversation growing animated. Harold gestured toward the store; his face flushed with anger.

"He's recruiting," Noble realized. "Turning today's confusion into tomorrow's opposition."

Jenny opened Rosa's ledger, new words flowing across the page in urgent script:

When the awakening becomes visible, the sleeping world takes notice. Those who profit from dreams deferred will not surrender without a fight. The real test approaches with outside eyes and official papers.

The words faded, but their warning remained.

Marcus finally drove away, his decision still unmade. Harold lingered, speaking into his phone with the intensity of a man calling for reinforcements.

Noble felt the keys pulse with warning rather than triumph. Today had been a beginning, not an ending. The store's magic was no longer hidden, and visibility brought dangers he was only starting to understand.

"What do we do now?" Sarah asked.

"We prepare," Noble said, watching Harold finally drive away. "For whatever Harold set in motion with those phone calls."

The evening light painted long shadows through Manning's

Hardware. But instead of peace, the shadows held the shapes of approaching storms.

JENNY WATCHED as Noble and Sarah navigated their inner pathways to find the truth, when nothing felt right. She felt the urge to reach for Eleanor's journal, which Sarah had seen in her camera bag. Flipping open to a random page, it read:

The horses still run between worlds, carrying messages between what is and what could be. Sometimes, in Cedar Springs' quietest moments, those who have learned to see catch glimpses of them.

Jenny reflecting on Eleanor's wisdom: some doorways are meant to be witnessed, not walked through. Some visions serve best when they teach us to value the world we stand in, not the worlds we might chase.

Noble's vision blurred as he read the final entry:

I see the doorway; I seem to be drawn toward it to follow them over the threshold. I see Sarah watching me, her eyes full of the same sight that terrifies her father. Noble thinks I'm chasing dreams, but I'm really chasing truth, the truth he'll have to face when the store finally awakens.

My beloved, practical man, you've spent so long measuring what can be counted that you've forgotten how to measure what counts. But the time's coming when you'll have to choose between the safety of your father's walls and the wild truth that runs in your blood.

Remember this: Transformation is about becoming something new when that moment arrives. It's also about finally being what we've always been and are meant to be. Eventually, you will accept your destiny and stop fighting it, for that only delays the inevitable, set in place by your grandfather when he built this store.

Noble's hands shook as he closed the journal. Through the window, Cedar Springs flickered between states of reality: what it was, what it could be, what it was afraid to become. Just like him.

He now realized that the threat to Cedar Springs was about more than regulation or stability. But really, it was about the choice Eleanor had seen: between remaining safely blind or accepting the cost of vision. Between his father's rigid certainty and his wife's wild truth, a world exists that he's finally starting to see.

The keys at his chest pulsed with this understanding. One sang of safety, of walls and measurements, and comfortable blindness. The other hummed with Eleanor's frequency, with Sarah's sight, with the wild magic that had always run in Manning blood.

"How do I know when I am ready?" he whispered to the quiet room.

Eleanor's voice seemed to answer from a faraway place, yet closer than his very skin:

No one ever does, my love. That's why it's called trans-formation.

Suddenly, Noble noticed the chemical scents of the darkroom that seemed to thicken, carrying memories of all the times Eleanor had tried to show him what lived between moments of ordinary sight. He could almost see her, bent over the developing trays, coaxing truth from shadows just as she'd tried to coax understanding from his practical heart.

Noble felt it in his blood, but something more profound was churning. The keys at his chest grew chill, responding to a distant threat that crept closer with each passing moment.

Rising from Eleanor's journal, he moved to the store's front window. The dusty glass revealed layers of possibility that seemed to be folding in on themselves, like flowers closing before the night.

Noble watched as frost spread across a windowpane in Cedar Springs. Soon, he would have to choose for himself: the store, the town, and everything that lived between moments of ordinary time.

The price of seeing was higher than he'd imagined, written in a currency his careful bookkeeping had never tracked. But the cost of remaining blind, he now understood, would bankrupt more than just his business.

It was time to step out of the safety of being blind to what was all around him; those who believed, those who witnessed the magic, and into whatever waited in the gathering darkness.

He felt restless now but determined to take a stand for what he realized was the only way out, the way of transformation, even if he didn't know what was on the other side, and neither did anyone else.

THE EVIDENCE OF FEAR

Something changed that day, nothing specific, but noticeable now to his awakened senses. Noble felt it early Tuesday morning, places where the store's magic seemed to thin, like watercolors bleeding into blank paper. Tools that had been singing felt muffled. Shadows that had danced grew tired.

"Something's different," Sarah said, lowering her camera with a frown. Through its lens, reality started to look ordinary. Wood, metal, and measurements again, as if the deeper layers were being systematically erased.

Jenny opened Rosa's ledger, its pages now showing gaps between stories, spaces where magic seemed to hesitate. "Gran wrote about this," she said softly. "About times when wonder is tested to weed out those not ready. The perfectly reasonable type of thinking that leaves no room for shadows or dreams."

The morning light through the windows carried a different quality, sharp and clean and somehow empty. Like hospital corridors. Like freshly erased chalkboards. Like everything Noble had once thought he wanted the store to be.

Stanford Blackwell had received Harold Whitaker's call just after his confrontation with Noble. The phone rang in his Seattle hotel room, where seventeen case files lay spread across his bed in precise order. Each file told the same story: magical emergence, community resistance to normalization, and eventual grateful acceptance of stability.

"Dr. Blackwell? This is Harold Whitaker, Cedar Springs Business Association. I read your article in the Times. We need your help before this situation destroys our town." Stanford opened file number eighteen while Harold described the "irregularities" spreading through Cedar Springs. The symptoms matched his predictive model exactly. Reality distortion originating from a central nexus point. Community leader displaying charismatic influence over rational thinking. Local businesses abandoning standard operating procedures in favor of "intuitive" practices.

"I'll be there tomorrow," Stanford said, already reaching for his travel kit. "Document everything. Photograph the violations. Record any unusual behaviors or statements. The state requires comprehensive evidence for intervention authorization."

His rental car contained documentation equipment calibrated to measure reality distortion, legal papers authorizing emergency stabilization procedures, and contact information for contractors specialized in rapid normalization. Seventeen successful interventions had taught him the importance of thorough preparation.

Harold met him at the town limits; his face etched with worry. They drove through streets where Stanford's trained eye noted the warning signs. Windows reflected light at impossible angles. Shadows lingered too long after their objects moved. The subtle wrongness that signaled an impending systematic collapse.

"It started at Manning's Hardware," Harold explained, his hands gripping the steering wheel. "Noble Manning. Three generations of solid business practices, then this. Tools move on their own. Customers find items they never came looking for. The whole downtown is infected."

Stanford nodded, making notes. The pattern held. Every intervention began with a single point of emergence, then spread through social networks until containment became impossible without external assistance.

At Harold's office, they spread evidence across the conference table. Stanford examined photographs of Manning's Hardware, noting the telltale energy distortions around doorframes and windows. Harold's documentation was thorough and professional. The man understood the stakes.

"Mrs. Chen's bakery has customers claiming her bread tastes like childhood memories," Harold continued. "Jack Thompson swears his wood sings to him. Maria Rodriguez grows flowers in colors that don't exist. It's mass hysteria disguised as wonder."

Stanford opened his laptop and began the preliminary assessment. The symptoms matched his database exactly. Cedar Springs displayed a Stage Three magical emergence, characterized by widespread reality distortion and active community participation. Without immediate intervention, the town would reach Stage Four within a matter of weeks. He had never seen a community recover from a Stage Four collapse.

"The residents need protection from themselves," Stanford said, reviewing Harold's documentation. "Magical emergence creates powerful psychological dependencies. People abandon rational thinking in favor of fantasy fulfillment. They interpret coincidence as a miracle, suggestion as a supernatural experience."

Harold's relief was visible. "So, you understand what we're facing."

"Seventeen towns have faced identical situations. All followed the same trajectory without intervention. Initial euphoria, followed by economic disruption, social break-down, and exodus. Communities scattered, families destroyed, local economies collapsed." Stanford closed the file. "But every town we've normalized has thanked us after-ward. Relief from the burden of impossible expectations."

He scheduled the emergency business association presenta-tion for the following evening. Forty-eight hours to document violations, prepare evidence, and present the community with a choice: accept normalization or face federal intervention.

"What about Manning himself?" Harold asked. "He's the center of this. The others follow his lead."

Stanford reviewed Noble's profile: a hardware store owner, recently widowed, with an adult daughter living out of state. The psychological markers suggested vulnerability to magical thinking. Grief often triggered susceptibility to wonder-based delusions.

Stanford collected his materials. "The business association meeting will go ahead, and I will introduce you to the members. They will understand the reasoning behind our actions, and you will be a welcome help. Maintaining community safety demands intervention, regardless of whether the source cooperates or resists," Harold explained.

That afternoon, Stanford walked the streets of Cedar Springs with clinical detachment. His equipment registered energy anomalies at seventeen different locations. Mrs. Chen's bakery was found to have dangerous levels of psychoactive compounds in her baked goods. Jack Thompson's workshop produced acoustic readings that violated known physics. Manning's Hardware pulsed with reality distortion patterns identical to those in his failed case studies. He photographed each violation systematically. The state required comprehensive documentation before authorizing emergency protocols. His report would provide governors with legal justification for immediate normalization procedures.

Back in his hotel room, Stanford drafted the assessment that would determine Cedar Springs' future. "Magical emergence following predictable parameters. Community displaying advanced symptoms of collective delusion. Recommend immediate implementation of Stability Protocol before permanent psychological damage occurs."

The words flowed with practiced efficiency. He had written identical reports seventeen times, each leading to successful community normalization. The pattern never varied: initial resistance, gradual acceptance, eventual gratitude for protection from their own dangerous fantasies.

His first communication was to the Governor's office, to whom he reported directly in situations like this. They demanded a full report of his progress, understanding that the spread of this "condition" would cause widespread panic and disruption.

His secure phone buzzed with updates from three state agencies. The governor demanded confirmation that the situation remained containable. Federal observers monitored his progress, authorized to escalate intervention if local methods proved insufficient.

Stanford reviewed his presentation materials one final time. Charts showing the economic collapse of unnormalized communities. Medical documentation of psychological damage from prolonged magical exposure. Success stories from seventeen towns that had chosen stability over wonder.

The Cedar Springs Chamber of Commerce meeting would offer the same choice. Accept his guidance toward rational operation, or face the consequences that have destroyed every other community foolish enough to believe in magic over measurement.

Nothing he had observed suggested Cedar Springs would prove different from any other case. The pattern held. The outcome was inevitable. By the end of the week, the town would join his list of successfully stabilized communities, grateful for salvation from their own impossible dreams.

Stanford closed his laptop and prepared for the next day's intervention. Seventeen successes had taught him exactly what to expect from number eighteen.

8

___

THE FATHER'S TRUTH

Noble felt the urgent need to be in the store now, where he could feel the power of the awakening world all around him. He had already returned home, but something he couldn't explain drove him to go back.

Noble stood alone in Manning's Hardware the night before the business association meeting. The keys at his chest had grown cold, almost burning with frozen fire against his skin. Through the windows, he watched Cedar Springs lose its magical sparkle like frost across a windowpane, systematically eroding magic wherever it touched.

"Dad?" Sarah's voice came from the doorway. She knew he would be there. She held Eleanor's camera, but its shutter wouldn't fire, as if refusing to see what was happening. "Something's wrong. The photographs... they're fading."

Noble turned to find his daughter holding out a stack of prints, all the transformative moments she'd captured since the awakening began. But the images were dissolving like sugar in the rain, magic bleeding out until only ordinary

109

scenes remained. He heard the front door close with its distinctive click; someone else had arrived.

"It's not just the photos," Jenny said, entering with Rosa's ledger clutched to her chest. "The stories are disappearing. Everything Gran ever wrote about the store's true nature..." She opened the book to show him pages where Rosa's flowing script was vanishing letter by letter.

The cold from the keys spread through Noble's chest, creating an icy void that consumed the magic he'd finally learned to embrace. He felt it trying to take more than just the wonder; it was draining his connection to Eleanor's memory, Sarah's gift, and everything that made Manning's Hardware more than just a store, as well as his own awakened mission.

"The resistance from Harold, that stranger he brought into our community," Sarah whispered, watching another photograph fade. "It's not just suppressing the magic. It's... erasing it. Like it never existed at all."

Noble staggered as the void in his chest expanded. Through increasingly gray vision, he saw the store's multiple layers of reality slowly fading, possibilities folding in on themselves like a flower dying in fast motion. Tools that had sung sounded sad in their muted tones. Wood that had whispered now lay mute.

"Dad!" Sarah caught him as his knees buckled. "What's happening?"

"The keys," he managed, his voice thick with ice. "They're trying to... protect the magic. But the cost..." He couldn't finish as another wave of cold crashed through him.

Jenny rushed forward with Rosa's ledger, but its pages now held only ordinary inventory counts. "This is more than just the magic of the store," she said, her grandmother's accent strong with fear. "It's about everything we are. Everything we could become."

Noble felt it then, the choice crystallizing in his frozen blood. Harold's way, his rational influence offered relief. He had to let go, accept the ordinary world, and return to simple commerce and precise measurements. The pain would stop, the cold would fade, and everything would be safe.

Sarah's hand found his, warm against his frost-chilled skin.

"Dad," she whispered, "Mom's last photograph. Look."

Through vision growing dark at the edges, Noble saw the print she held: Eleanor's final shot of those empty meadows. But now he understood what she'd been trying to show him. The empty spaces weren't empty at all. They were pregnant with possibility, waiting for someone brave enough to believe in what couldn't be measured.

The keys burned intensely, amplifying more of his warmth, life, and connection to wonder. Harold's way pressed closer, promising relief if he would surrender, accept the simpler reality, and stop believing...

Noble gathered his remaining strength and pushed himself to his feet. "Your mother," he said through chattering teeth. "She was running toward what reality could become, and she tried to show me too, but I wasn't ready."

The keys flared with sudden warmth, responding to this truth. Sarah caught Noble's eye and felt something tear loose inside him. The last of his doubt melted into understanding the foundation of who he'd been. In that moment of shared recognition, Sarah sensed her own walls beginning to crumble.

She moved through the aisles, remembering how she'd once arranged tools by their tones rather than their functions. She'd spent years convincing herself that those memories were childhood fantasies, forcing herself to see only surface reality.

But every photograph she curated whispered to her of more profound truths, and every artist she worked with somehow found their way to her gallery with questions about seeing beyond the obvious. The gift hadn't left her; it had simply waited, growing more potent in its silence.

Standing here now, in the place she'd tried so hard to forget, Sarah realized she had never truly left. She had merely been waiting, like these tools, like this store, like Cedar Springs itself, for the moment when remembering became easier than it had been before forgetting.

The pain was enormous, a scouring fire that burned away everything he'd built himself upon.

He heard Sarah cry out and felt Jenny attempt to support him, but they seemed to come from a great distance.

The store's reality rippled around him as he fell, as the old Noble Manning - the man of measurements and certainties - was gone.

But something new began in that death, in that absolute surrender to transformation.

Noble opened eyes that saw differently. The keys at his chest no longer burned with either fire or ice; they sang with completion. The store's magic: undefeated, had gone deeper, now rooted in wonder and wisdom.

"Dad?" Sarah's voice trembled. "Your eyes..."

Jenny gasped. "Like Rosa's, when she knew something that couldn't be unknown."

Noble slowly regained his balance, steady now, transformed. His eyes blazed with conviction of what he knew to be true… and real. Finally, he could see.

The cold was gone, replaced by an understanding that ran deep within the soul. Harold's influence still pressed against the windows, but it could no longer touch what had become part of him.

"The business association meets tomorrow," he said, his voice echoing his father's strength and Eleanor's vision. "But the real meeting has already happened... right here, right now."

Sarah's camera stirred in her hands, its lens clearing. Jenny opened Rosa's ledger to find new words, appearing in ink that looked like liquid gold. Cedar Springs seemed to hold its breath through the windows, waiting to see what this reborn Noble Manning would choose.

He touched the keys at his chest, feeling how they'd changed, how he changed, and not just physical objects around him; they no longer mattered. He crossed over, no longer entirely identifying with the physical 3D world; now, that world lived inside a much bigger vision of the multidimensional, unseen world.

It was a world far more beautiful, more stable, and entirely real; now he had to show the others. In his own awakening, as the truth surged through his body and soul, he could hardly fathom why anyone would desire anything else.

"Your mother knew," he told Sarah softly.

"But at what cost? I almost lost everything, forever. But now…" Noble searched for words to match what he now fully understood, but remained speechless.

"It's becoming something new," Sarah finished, understanding blooming in her eyes. "Even when the becoming feels like breaking."

Noble nodded, feeling the last pieces of his old self disappear, making space for who he'd become. Manning's Hardware breathed with him, its magic running through his blood as much as through its walls.

The night pressed against the windows, but now its darkness felt like a possibility rather than a threat. Tomorrow would bring its own challenges, but Noble faced them as someone new: a man who had died to certainty and been reborn to wonder as an awakened being. In this moment, Noble was sure that he would never go back, and yet he wasn't sure what he was moving toward.

Looking over at Sarah, he saw the glow around her; he saw the depth of her wisdom and realized that she had been the master teacher to her student-father, just as Jenny had been to her, just as Rosa had been to both of them. Just as her mother had been for her, and now finally… for Noble.

It was time to show Cedar Springs what transformation truly meant.

The Cedar Springs Business Association emergency meeting was scheduled for 7:00 a.m. at the Grand Hotel.

Still, Noble's real trial began hours before, in the quietest corner of Manning's Hardware.

He looked around and realized that Jenny had been there for

hours. He was still reeling from his transformation and the flood of realizations that continued even now.

He felt drawn to the back room, where he searched for an old inventory list. He noticed a crack at the seams between the walls and floor, where light met darkness. Instinctively, he touched the dust-covered wall, causing a hidden door to swing open.

It was his father's private office, precisely as it had been left fifteen years ago, yet somehow wholly transformed. Shocked, he thought it had been converted to warehouse space in the last remodel, but now it felt like a hidden gift waiting for him to find it.

The evening moonlight streamed through dusty windows, glinting off brass fixtures that seemed to hold more than mere age. His father's old desk calendar still displayed June 15, 1998, the last day he had sat in that leather chair, yet the date now shimmered with new possibilities: other Junes, other moments when paths diverged, and choices resonated through time.

The scent hit him first, leather and wood, yes, but underneath that, something else. The sharp tang of his father's disappointment when Noble had suggested carrying Rosa's "fancy foreign herbs" alongside the garden supplies.

When Eleanor wanted to display local artists' work between the tools, arguments about "proper business practices" arose bitterly. The heavy musk of traditions maintained the familiar and discarded the possibilities.

Seeing the glow of the open door in the storeroom's distance, Sarah found him standing in the doorway as reality rippled around him. Her camera hung silent at her throat, but her eyes held that same seeing-beyond-seeing that had made Eleanor both magical and mysterious.

"Mom used to say this office felt like a tomb," she said softly, "preserving something that needed to change."

Noble touched the keys on his chest. Both hummed with recognition, but in different ways. The familiar one resonated with decades of Manning tradition, while the ancient one sang of what could be.

"I realize the real test comes after the association meeting, right?" he asked Sarah, though he already knew the answer.

"Harold isn't the one you need to face." Sarah's voice carried echoes of Eleanor's gentle wisdom. "He's just a reflection of…"

The temperature in the room dropped suddenly. The lights flickered, though the store's power had nothing to do with Cedar Springs' electrical grid anymore.

And there, in his father's chair, a shadow began to gather substance.

The shadow of Thomas Manning Jr. took form slowly, like ink spreading through water. At first, it was just an impression: the straight spine, the squared shoulders, the unbending certainty.

Noble had spent his life trying to emulate him. Then details emerged. The wire-rimmed glasses, the perfectly knotted tie, the ledger eternally open on the desk before him.

"All these years," his father's voice whispered, carrying that familiar note of disappointment that had shaped Noble's choices for decades. "All these years, I have upheld order, maintained structure, and created something real. And now you would discard it for fairy tales?"

The air in the office thickened with memory. Noble could smell his father's pipe tobacco, even though he hadn't smoked in that final year. He could hear the scratch of a pen on paper as profits were counted, losses measured, and everything reduced to what could be quantified.

Sarah took a step forward, but Noble raised a hand. This confrontation had been waiting since he was a boy, listening to Rosa's stories while his father's frown cast shadows over wonder.

"We weren't building something real," Noble said, his voice steady despite the trembling in his chest. "We were hiding something real behind ledgers and lists. The store was always more than numbers, and you knew that."

The shadow that wore his father's face hardened. "Numbers don't lie, son. Numbers don't tell stories. Numbers…"

"Numbers are just one way of measuring truth…"

Noble interrupted. The keys at his chest hummed stronger now, their warmth spreading through him like dawn through darkness. "Rosa knew that. Eleanor knew it. Even you knew it, deep down."

Noble saw through the stern mask now, recognizing the cost of his father's chosen blindness. He remembered the day he had discovered his father's private journal hidden behind the store's ledgers.

Pages filled with drawings of tools that glowed, notes about wood that whispered stories, and in the margins, time and again: *I must protect him from this. Better that he should see only surfaces than suffer the weight of seeing everything.* His father had chosen ignorance as a shield, believing it would spare his son from the burden he carried.

The office seemed to pulse with opposing powers, the rigid order his father had imposed, and the wild possibility that had always lived in the store's bones.

The papers on the desk began to shift. Some showed columns of figures, while others revealed the stories hidden between the lines.

"Rosa Martinez," his father's shadow almost spat the name, "filling your head with nonsense about tools that choose their owners. Eleanor with her empty photographs. Sarah, with her strange questions. I thought at least you understood what was real."

But as he spoke, the shadow's edges began to waver. Through his father's form, Noble caught glimpses of other moments:

A young Thomas Manning Jr. watched his own father measure lumber with a ruler that sometimes measured dreams instead of inches.

A teenage Thomas found strange messages in the grain of the wood, then deliberately looked away. A man choosing certainty over wonder, measurement over magic, fear over transformation.

The words of time floated through the air and slowly sank as Noble realized now that he had followed another's instincts instead of his own.

"You saw it too," Noble whispered, understanding flowing like spring water. "You felt it. The store's magic. The possibility. But you were afraid."

"I was practical!" The shadow's voice boomed, but now Noble could hear the tremor beneath the thunder. "Someone had to be practical! Someone had to maintain order!"

"Order isn't the opposite of magic," Sarah said softly. Her camera lifted almost of its own accord. "Grandpa, let me show you what you couldn't let yourself see."

The camera's shutter clicked, and reality rippled like a stone thrown into still water. Suddenly, the office held multiple versions of Thomas Manning Sr., the stern businessman, yes, but also the boy who'd once dreamed of building wonders.

The young man who'd given Rosa a job because something in her eyes spoke to something in his soul: the father who'd watched his son's wonder with a mixture of fear and longing.

"The store remembers," Noble said, gentler now. "It remembers everything we try to forget. Every dream we set aside. Every magic we denied. Every possibility we were too afraid to embrace."

The shadow in Thomas Manning Jr.'s chair flickered like a candle flame in the wind. Through its wavering form, Noble could see decades of choice and consequence; his father had always chosen ledgers over legends, measurement over mystery, and safety over possibility.

"The numbers protected us," his father insisted, but his voice now carried echoes of other emotions: longing, regret, and the bittersweet taste of dreams deferred.

"The structure... the systems..."

"Protected us from what?" Noble asked softly. The keys at his chest hummed with a harmony he'd never noticed before, a kind of resonant ringing that he felt throughout his entire body.

Like his father's ledgers and Rosa's stories. Like Eleanor's camera and Sarah's sight. Like tradition and transformation dancing together in the space between heartbeats.

"From..." The shadow seemed to struggle, its edges blurring. "From..."

"From wonder?" Sarah suggested gently. Through her camera's lens, the office filled with soft light, revealing years of magical moments his father had pretended not to see:

Tools that find their proper owners without being shown.

Seeds sprout according to stories rather than seasons.

Rosa's organizational system somehow always led customers to exactly what they needed, even when they didn't know what that was.

"From possibility," Noble explained, understanding blooming in his chest like dawn. "From the responsibility of seeing what could be, instead of just what was."

The shadow that was his father seemed to sink deeper into the chair, but its substance had changed.

Now, it looked less like the imposing Thomas Manning Sr. and more like the man Noble barely remembered from earliest childhood. Now, he saw the one who had sometimes smiled at Rosa's stories and kept Eleanor's strange photographs in his desk drawer.

The reluctant father who had watched his son's wonder with hunger in his eyes and the love of a father for a son who never lost sight of his own dreams.

"I thought I was protecting the legacy," the shadow whispered. "The Manning name. The family business."

"The legacy, dad, was more about possibility than numbers." Noble stepped forward, both keys singing against his chest. "About transformation… about helping people build more than just houses and gardens; it is about assisting them to build dreams, hope, and new beginnings... to face their fears and move forward into the unknown. Don't you see, Dad? We held the dreams of the entire town and nurtured them into reality even when no one else saw the possibilities. Isn't that what we were really meant to do?"

Sarah's camera clicked again, and this time, the image it captured seemed to hang between them:

Three generations of Manning men, each standing at their own crossroads.

Noble's grandfather chose to hire Rosa despite the town's prejudices. His father had turned away from magic, but he could never entirely forget it. Noble himself stood now between what was and what could be.

The shadow began to fade, like mist becoming morning dew, transforming rather than vanishing, changing form rather than ceasing to exist.

"The business association meeting," his father's voice came one last time, softer now, almost gentle. "Harold Whitaker and this intruder he's summoned..."

"I'm not worried, Dad, I know what the real challenge is now," Noble finished. "The real challenge was always in this room, in this choice between measuring life and living it."

The shadow smiled: the first genuine smile Noble could remember seeing on his father's face in decades. Then, it dissolved completely, leaving behind a scent like spring rain and pine needles as the past slowly merged with the present.

Sarah lowered her camera.

"Dad," she said softly, "look at the desk."

New words were written in a familiar flowing script where his father's ledger had lain unchanged for fifteen years. Rosa's handwriting shimmered like starlight on the water as Noble and Sarah leaned forward to read:

> *The deepest caves we enter are not carved from stone but built from fear... fear of change, wonder, and of becoming more than we were taught to be.*
> *Yet these caves hold our greatest treasures: the forgotten dreams of those who came before us, waiting to be remembered. For in remembering their magic, we free ourselves and all those who shaped us through their unspoken longings.*

The words faded slowly, like footprints in the sand at the tide's turn. Outside, the night sky glowed with an intensity not seen in years, painting the town in colors that suggested both memory and possibility, the past and future.

The business association meeting would start soon, but Noble knew that it was just another threshold to cross, another opportunity to choose between measuring life and living it fully.

While Noble faced his father's ghost in the hidden office, Jenny sat at Rosa's kitchen table with the ledger open before her. The pages flickered between stories and blank whiteness, reflecting the battle between memory and forgetting happening at the store.

She felt Noble's struggle through the connection Rosa had taught her to maintain with Manning's Hardware. Her sight gift let her sense the store's emotional weather: the cold pressure of old shame, the heat of transformation fighting against rigid tradition, the electric tension of a soul choosing between safety and truth.

It was time to go home, reflect on the evening's revelations, and get ready for the challenges ahead. It was time to regroup and prepare for tomorrow.

Later that evening, Ruby called from college, her voice tight with concern. "Mom, something's wrong. I can feel it from here. The quantum equations I've been working on, the ones about parallel realities… are all collapsing into single outcomes. Like possibilities are being forced to choose."

Jenny understood. Her daughter's scientific sight and her own inherited wisdom were different expressions of the same gift. Ruby could measure what Jenny could feel: the moment when multiple futures narrowed to a single path, when transformation either succeeded or utterly failed.

"Your grandfather Noble is remembering who he really is," Jenny told Ruby. "But first, he has to face who his father taught him to be."

She opened Rosa's ledger to pages she had never seen before. Her grandmother's handwriting appeared as she watched:

Your sacred gift carries responsibility beyond arrangement. When others face their deepest fears, we hold space for their becoming.

Jenny learned this through single motherhood, through nights when Ruby's cries mixed with her own tears. She knows how to remain steady when others shake apart."

Jenny felt the truth of those words. She had developed strength through struggle, wisdom through sleepless nights, and found balance between work and motherhood. Rosa's gift had grown in her through necessity, becoming something more practical and sustainable than pure intuition.

The temperature in her kitchen dropped. Through the window, she could see Manning's Hardware in the distance, its windows flickering with unnatural light. She placed her hands flat on the table and sent her intention toward the store: steadiness to ground Noble's transformation, clarity to cut through old confusion, love to warm the cold spaces where fear had lived too long.

The ledger's pages settled into readable text. Rosa's wisdom flowed across them:

> *Every transformation needs witnesses who remember*
> *the truth when the one changing forgets.*

Her purpose right now is to anchor Noble's becoming in practical love, to hold space for his return to himself.

Jenny maintained her vigil through the dark hours, sending strength across the sleeping town to a man learning to embrace the magic his family had always carried. When dawn broke, she felt the shift: Noble had chosen becoming over remaining, wonder over fear.

Noble would need her steady presence as he integrated his awakening with his daily responsibilities, and soon the town meeting would become his greatest challenge. Jenny closed the ledger and prepared to help him build foundations strong enough to support his transformed sight.

For Noble, it was time to remember who he, the store, and the town had always been meant to be.

9

THE PRICE OF WONDER

Stanford Blackwell sat in his Grand Hotel room, the night before the morning meeting, surrounded by files that told stories of systematic failure. Seventeen towns. Seventeen interventions. Seventeen communities saved from the destructive spiral of unchecked magical emergence. The documentation spread across the hotel room dresser told the same story repeatedly: wonder without wisdom destroyed everything it touched.

He opened the Millbrook, Vermont, file first; Diana Wells' hometown. The photographs showed Main Street before the awakening: prosperous shops, stable families, predictable commerce. The after images revealed empty storefronts, foreclosure notices, and a community scattered by dreams that had turned toxic.

Mrs. Wells's incident report lay beneath the photos. Margaret Wells, sixty-three, was found at the base of Miller's Bridge after following bread that promised to lead her home to Ireland. The medical examiner discovered hallucinogenic compounds in her system, produced by uncontrolled fermentation in memory-laden loaves.

Stanford touched the file with steady fingers. He'd arrived in Millbrook six weeks too late. The normalization process took three months, leaving behind a town that functioned but no longer dreamed. Diana had joined his team afterward, driven by grief to prevent other families from suffering similar losses.

The following file: Cascade Heights, Oregon - a café where coffee carried visions of possible futures. Twelve customers were hospitalized after consuming beverages that induced psychotic episodes. The barista, convinced her gift was helping people, had continued serving prophetic drinks until three patrons attempted suicide, believing the futures they'd seen were inevitable.

Stanford reviewed his intervention notes: "Café normalized within two weeks. Owner relocated. A community memorial garden was established on the site where the building once stood. Residents report satisfaction with increased safety measures."

Each file contained similar patterns. Musical instruments that played themselves, driving listeners to sing out loud in public. Flowers that bloomed in impossible colors, triggering fits of unbridled exuberance. Antique furniture that revealed the memories of previous owners, causing identity confusion and feelings of abandonment within the family.

His protocols had evolved through challenging experience. The Stability Enhancement Process began with documentation of violations, continued with community education about the dangers of uncontrolled emergence, and concluded with systematic reality reinforcement. The success rate approached 100%.

His secure phone buzzed with an encrypted message: "Federal oversight intervention enforced if normalization is delayed beyond twenty-four hours. Governor requests confirmation of timeline adherence."

Stanford typed his response with mechanical precision: "Proceeding as scheduled. Protocols will be implemented following business association approval."

He closed the laptop and prepared for the meeting. His presentation was ready, documenting violations, safety incidents, and a projected collapse timeline. The same materials that had convinced seventeen previous communities to accept normalization.

Stanford adjusted his tie and gathered his files. Tomorrow's contractors were already positioned outside town. The normalization equipment sat ready for deployment. Within forty-eight hours, Cedar Springs would join his list of successfully stabilized communities.

The next morning at 6:00 am sharp, Stanford picked up his briefcase. He headed toward the business association meeting, where he would do what he'd done seventeen times before: save a community from its own dangerous dreams.

THE SHORT WALK from Noble's Hardware to the Grand Hotel felt like moving between dimensions. Noble knew that everything entrusted to him by the last two generations was at risk, but he felt no fear. It was time for the new world to begin by recognizing the old world's gifts.

The meeting room at the top of the winding wooden staircase

held no actual magic, but it pulsed with other kinds of power: old money, established influence, and fear.

The kind of authority that came from decades of deciding what Cedar Springs would and wouldn't become. Noble felt it the moment he entered: the weight of tradition masquerading as progress, the suffocation of wonder beneath the guise of practicality.

Harold Whitaker stood at the head of the long mahogany table, his tablet gleaming like armor in the chandelier light. The other board members, twelve of Cedar Springs' most prominent business owners, sat in their usual places. Their faces were set in expressions that suggested the verdict had been decided before Noble arrived.

A guest had been seated next to Harold, and when Noble realized it was Stanford Blackwell, the man who had written the article Harold had shown him, a chill ran down his spine, and the room had become eerily still.

But Noble wasn't alone. Sarah stood to his right with Eleanor's camera ready. Jenny was to his left, and Rosa's ledger was held like a shield. And behind them, filling the observer seats usually left empty at these meetings, sat their unexpected allies:

Mrs. Chen was still covered with baking flour from the morning prep work. Jack Thompson's hands, gleaming with traces of starlight sawdust. Maria Rodriguez, with her stained apron, painted the air with the colors of life itself. Marcus from the bank sat in the middle, rather than in his usual place at the board table.

The keys at Noble's chest hummed with different songs. The familiar one recognized the power in the room; the ancient one sensed a deeper current beneath the surface.

Sarah hoped the room would show its true nature: a battle-field where wonder and measurement would finally face each other directly.

Harold cleared his throat, signaling that the meeting was about to begin. The meeting room felt unnaturally still. Even the familiar creak of the old oak chairs seemed muted as Stanford Blackwell stood before Cedar Springs' assembled leaders. His crisp suit and perfect posture starkly contrasted with the small-town informality of their surroundings.

"We have a special guest with us today, a man who has encountered the type of… disruptions we are experiencing here, in multiple towns and cities. Meet Stanford Blackwell, who has traveled a long distance to be with us today. Mr. Blackwell, the floor is yours."

Thank you, Harold, for the invitation to visit with all of you here in Cedar Springs. What's happening to your town isn't magic," Stanford's voice carried quiet authority. "It's a pattern I've seen before that always ends the same way." He placed a leather briefcase on the polished table, each movement precise and measured.

"Let me show you what happened in New Hope, Oregon."

Stanford's presentation was flawless. His slides told the story of another small town that had "awakened." His graphs showed initial business growth, community excitement, and a sense of possibility. Then came the decline: insurance claims, safety violations, and financial instability.

"They started with simple things," Stanford continued, his voice gentle with understanding. "A bakery whose bread carried memories of home. A carpenter whose wood spoke of future possibilities. Sound familiar?"

Mrs. Chen clutched her apron, flour dust no longer sparkling with possibility but just... dust. Jack Thompson's calloused hands, still bearing traces of luminescent sawdust, curled into uncertain fists.

"Three months later." Stanford clicked to the next slide. New Hope's main street looked like this: empty storefronts, fore-closure notices, and a community center reduced to concrete foundations. "They forgot that dreams need solid ground. That wonder without wisdom destroys everything it touches."

Noble's mind wandered as Stanford droned on about how dangerous this "magic" really was; his attention was drawn to the sky.

Cedar Springs appeared changed through the boardroom windows of the Grand Hotel. The magic that had started to flow through its streets now flickered like a candle in a strong wind.

"The town feels wrong," Sarah whispered, lowering her camera. The photos showed only ordinary tools, shadows, and... life. "It's like it's forgetting how to dream."

Jenny held Rosa's ledger, and its pages now showed only inventory counts where stories had danced. "Gran wrote about times like this," she said softly. "When fear makes people choose safety over possibility."

Stanford delivered his presentation with practiced ease, each word carefully chosen.

"Manning's Hardware has become the center of something dangerous." He displayed photographs of failed businesses, broken dreams, and shattered lives from other towns. "Noble Manning is a good man," Stanford acknowledged, his voice filled with genuine respect. "Like his father before him, he has been a pillar of this community. But something has changed. You have all felt it. The way tools seem to choose their owners. Shadows that move when they shouldn't. Wood that whispers of forests long gone."

The room grew quieter, and business owners exchanged uneasy glances. They'd all experienced it: the magic threaded through their daily work made everything feel more alive and meaningful. But under Stanford's steady gaze, those experiences began to feel foolish, even irresponsible.

"Three weeks ago," Stanford continued, "Mrs. Chen's bread started carrying memories." He turned to her gently. "How many customers have complained of unexpected allergic reactions because they were too caught up in the memories to check the ingredients?"

Mrs. Chen's face flushed as she muttered, "There had been a few incidents, nothing serious, but..."

"Jack Thompson." Stanford's voice remained kind. "Your saw slipped last Tuesday. Thirty years of experience, yet you were distracted by starlight in the wood grain. Nearly lost two fingers."

Jack looked down at his bandaged hand, the wonder of his awakened workshop suddenly feeling dangerous rather than miraculous.

Before the meeting at the store, Sarah remembered walking between shelves that no longer whispered stories. *Something's happening to the town,* she thought, her camera capturing only ordinary moments now. *It's like everyone's choosing to forget.*

Jenny's fingers traced words in Rosa's ledger that appeared to fade even as she read them. "They're scared," she said softly. "Stanford's making them fear their own magic."

Noble felt it, too. The doubt crept in like evening shadows. Every incident Stanford had mentioned was true. Every risk he'd identified was real. The keys at his chest grew colder still, their certainty wavering.

Cedar Springs seemed to flatten, its layers of possibility compressing into simple reality. Mrs. Chen's bread became just bread. Jack's tools seemed to flatten into just being tools. The print shop's ink carried nothing but words.

"We need to act now," Stanford told the assembled leaders. "Before someone follows visions too far, as Eleanor Manning did. Before another town tears itself apart chasing dreams never meant to be real." There was a gasp among the members, all remembering the loss of Eleanor and Noble's horrible and sudden loss.

He opened another folder, meticulously organizing documents. "I've developed what I call the Stability Protocol, a systematic approach to helping communities return to solid ground and protect themselves from the dangers of unchecked transformation."

Harold looked at the papers and then around the room at his fellow business owners. People he'd known all his life were now caught between wonder and fear.

Stanford watched the board members' faces as his presentation came to a close. The familiar pattern should have emerged: concern replacing curiosity, fear overtaking wonder, practical minds accepting the necessity of intervention. Instead, he saw something unexpected in their expressions.

Harold Whitaker studied the photographs of failed businesses from other towns. "These violations you've documented," Harold asked. "The accidents and incidents, how long after the awakening did they occur?"

"Typically, within the first month," Stanford replied, consulting his notes. "The pattern is consistent across all seventeen cases."

"But Cedar Springs has been... different... for six weeks now," Mrs. Chen said, her flour-dusted hands resting calmly in her lap. "Where are our accidents? Our violations?"

Stanford was prepared. He pulled out his Cedar Springs documentation, the incidents he'd catalogued during his three-day observation period. Mrs. Chen's allergic reactions. Jack's saw accident. Harold's printing press irregularities.

But as he read the reports aloud, Mrs. Chen began to object. "Customers had experienced mild reactions, not the severe poisoning documented in Vermont. Jack's injury was a minor cut, not the traumatic amputation that had occurred in Oregon," she insisted.

"The incidents here are..." Stanford paused, reviewing his own handwriting. "Possibly even worse than those I've discovered in those other towns. The readings are off the charts."

Noble leaned forward. "What if the difference isn't in the magic itself, but in how we're choosing to work with it?"

Stanford's jaw tightened. "Magic is magic, Mr. Manning. It follows predictable patterns regardless of human intentions."

Harold noticed the disbelief and denial in the other members. he turned to Noble and faced him. "We should at least discuss this with Noble," he said, but his voice lacked conviction.

Before Noble could respond, Stanford gently said, "Noble Manning is too close to this situation. Like his father before him, he's trying to contain something that can't be contained. But unlike his father, he's losing control. And the price of that loss could be everything you've built, everything you are."

Harold turned to him. "Noble, what do you have to say about this?"

Harold asked as everyone on that side of the room sank into their chairs. Noble collected his thoughts and was about to address the room when Harold interrupted. "Before you respond, let's look at the facts."

Harold tapped his tablet screen, and images of Manning's Hardware appeared on the wall behind him. Images of irregularities and anomalies, strange lights, and moving inventory all seemed to be non-standard by any means.

"The evidence is clear," Harold said, determined to move forward quickly and return Cedar Springs to normal.

Sarah raised her camera, its shutter clicking like destiny dealing cards. The chandelier light rippled, and suddenly, the meeting room itself began to remember.

A slight hue of color seeped into the room, like streams flowing in lazy circles.

The mahogany table seemed to recall its origins as a living tree; its growth rings told stories of seasons and dreams. The leather chairs seemed to remember being wild things, running under open skies. Even the air conditioning whispered of wind, weather, and wild possibilities.

Board members shifted uncomfortably as their surroundings came to life.

Some looked almost hungry, like old Pete from the garage, as if tasting something they'd craved without knowing. Others, led by Harold, gripped their seats tighter as if afraid this tide of transformation might carry them away.

"This is exactly what I'm talking about," Stanford Blackwell said, but his voice had lost its certainty. "This... disruption. This chaos. This isn't business!"

"Isn't it?" Mrs. Chen stood, and the flour dust around her painted pictures in the air, stories of bread that carried the taste of homeland, of recipes that fed more than bodies. "What do you think business is, Mr. Blackwell? Just numbers? Just profit?"

Jack Thompson rose next, his sawdust casting constellations on the polished floor. "Every beam I've ever placed, every joint I've ever fitted, they all held dreams and weight. We used to know that in Cedar Springs."

Harold stood up, trying to disrupt the overwhelming rise of those convinced of the transformation's positive effect on the town's people.

"The Real Reason We Are Here…Progress," Harold tried again with Stanford at his side, clutching his folders.

But Maria Rodriguez was already standing, her flower-covered hands trailing colors that spoke of growth and renewal.

"Progress? You mean tearing down the old to build the new?" she said. "It's remembering why we built things in the first place. Why we're here at all."

The keys at Noble's chest sang in harmony with these truths. He felt power gathering in the room, unlike money or influence, but something far older: the power of transformation and the power of becoming, the power of… awakening.

He now understood why his father had built such rigid systems, not to deny the magic, but to give it structure. Each careful measurement had been a foundation for wonder to build upon. "My father knew," he said softly to the assembled board. "He created these systems to protect the magic until we were ready to remember it properly, not contain them."

"Manning's Hardware is changing," Noble said, watching the images on the wall continue their revelation. "It's remembering just like the whole town is remembering. What we were. What we could be."

"This is ridiculous," Harold snapped. "We're here to vote on…"

"On what?" Jenny opened Rosa's ledger, and stories rose from its pages like steam from ancient ceremonial tea. "On whether to allow hope and possibilities back into Cedar Springs? On whether to let people remember that commerce was once about more than profit?"

"On whether to keep pretending we don't see what we see?" Sarah asked, her camera capturing truth after truth. "Feel what we feel? Know what we know?"

As the words left her lips, Jenny felt the weight of her own journey in them. She clutched Rosa's ledger closer, feeling its warmth against her chest.

She remembered her first days at Manning's, when she was just a teenager desperate for work. She was unaware that the store had called her, as surely as it had called her grandmother. Over the years, she'd moved from stocking shelves to arranging inventory by intention rather than category, from counting cash to measuring the flow of possibilities.

Noble had seen her as a reliable helper, and Sarah had recognized her as an ally, but Rosa had known from the beginning that Jenny wasn't just an employee. She was a bridge between the old magic and the new, between Rosa's ancient wisdom and Cedar Springs' awakened future. Every customer she'd guided to precisely what they needed, every tool she'd helped find its rightful owner, had prepared her for this moment of becoming.

The ledger pulsed with life in her hands, and Jenny lifted her chin to face Harold with newfound certainty. We must protect the store's magic; she must claim her role as its keeper!

Noble stepped forward, both keys humming against his chest. The chandelier light glowed more brightly, now surrounding him, casting shadows that spoke of choices and chances, of crossroads and transformations.

"I move for a different kind of vote," he said quietly. "Not on whether to stop the change because you can't stop it any more than you can stop spring from following winter. But whether Cedar Springs will fight its awakening or finally remember what it was always meant to be."

The silence that followed Noble's words was heavy with the weight of transformation.

Through the hotel's windows, he could see that Cedar Springs seemed to hold its breath.

The morning light painted the town in colors that suggested memory and possibility, as if multiple versions of reality were overlapping, waiting to see which would become true.

Harold stood frozen as board members began to shift in their seats. Stanford Blackwell collected and neatly arranged his folders in front of the board without looking up, without comment, and with a sense of loss.

Old Pete from the garage was the first to move, pulling something from his pocket: a worn spark plug that gleamed with more than just metal.

"Been keeping this for thirty years," he said, his gruff voice rough with emotion. "The first part I ever fixed that felt like it fixed something in the person, too. The customer drove in with a broken-down car and a broken-down life. Left with both running sweeter."

He placed the sparkplug on the table, but it seemed to float above the surface instead. "Been pretending ever since that it was just good business. But it was more, much more, wasn't it?"

Mrs. Chen stepped forward, placing a small loaf of bread beside the spark plug. Steam rose from it despite being hours old, carrying scents of home, healing, and hope. Jack revealed a wood shaving that spiraled with starlight. Maria contributed a single flower blooming with colors beyond the ordinary spectrum.

One by one, Cedar Springs' business owners revealed their own special magic. The pharmacist's measuring cups sometimes held wellness instead of just pills. The tailor's thread that stitched confidence into suits. The jeweler's loupe showed more than flaws but futures.

"You are all hallucinating. This is exactly what to expect when this anomaly, what you call magic, appears. Recognize it now before it's too late. You saw the photos of those other towns; we don't want to end up like that!" His voice was

cracking with both fear and determination to stop all
this now.

"We didn't let ourselves know," the pharmacist said gently.
"Just like you don't let yourself remember what your father's
printing press used to do, how sometimes the words it printed
changed lives, not just paper."

Harold's tablet vibrated gently in his hands, its screen flickering to life one last time. But instead of spreadsheets and
projections, it showed old photographs from when Whitaker
Printing had been more than just a copy shop. He looked
down, then turned the tablet over, placing it on the mahogany
table, trying to ignore what was there, realizing that he, too,
was "infected" and would have to be more aware of his own
feelings.

Noble stood and faced the room. The weight of three generations pressed against his shoulders, but his voice remained
steady.

"You know me. You've known my family for over a century.
My grandfather built this store when Cedar Springs was
barely a crossroads. My father kept it running through depression and war. In all that time, have the Mannings ever led this
community astray?"

He paused, letting his words settle. "Mr. Blackwell shows you
photographs of failed towns, businesses that collapsed
chasing impossible dreams. But look around this room. Look
at yourselves. Mrs. Chen, your bread now feeds more than
just bodies. Jack, your workshop hums with purpose you'd
forgotten. Harold, your press prints words that matter again."

Noble's voice grew stronger. "These aren't failures waiting to
happen. These are gifts you've always carried, now finally
given permission to breathe. Stanford speaks of safety, of

proven methods. But what has his safety preserved? Towns that function but no longer dream. Communities that survive but forget why they wanted to live."

He met each board member's eyes. "I'm not asking you to choose recklessness over reason. I'm asking you to choose becoming over remaining. To trust what you've experienced over what you've been told to fear."

The room held its breath. Through the windows, Cedar Springs waited.

"The question isn't whether magic is dangerous. The question is whether we dare to learn how to live with wonder instead of despite it."

Stanford Blackwell stood, and the room became silent.

"What you are experiencing now is the charismatic plea of a man who has lost control. Not only of his business but of his family, the trouble this 'magic' has caused, and the future problems for all of you if we don't stop it now. If you care about the future, you must restore stability to your town before it looks like this." He held up a poster-sized photo of the empty streets, abandoned storefronts, and empty homes.

"The future isn't separate from the past," Noble said softly. Both keys hummed against his chest, their song growing stronger. "Real progress is knowing the risks and remembering why we needed it in the first place."

The chandelier light seemed to pulse, and suddenly, the room was full of shadows that weren't shadows but the choices of everyone who'd ever stood at this same crossroad before.

Noble's father and grandfather. Rosa in her younger days. Eleanor with her camera of truth. All the keepers of Cedar

Springs' magic watched as the town remembered what it had tried to forget.

Marcus was confused. Years of practical decision-making, all for a good reason, were all of a sudden in doubt. There was solid logic in what Stanford Blackwell proposed, so why did he feel conflicted?

Suddenly, he felt scared. What if he were infected with this magic stuff and somehow blinded to the truth and safety he's always cherished?

"So," Noble said into that deafening silence, "shall we vote?"

Harold's hands trembled slightly as he consulted his tablet. "The motion before us is clear," he said, his voice carrying forced authority. "Implementation of preliminary safety protocols pending comprehensive study of... anomalous activities... in Cedar Springs businesses."

Stanford nodded approvingly. "A measured approach. Exactly what saved seventeen other communities."

"Those who support the motion?" Harold called.

Six hands rose: Harold himself, two other shop owners who'd remained silent throughout the evening, the insurance agent, the bank president, and, surprisingly, Dr. Martinez from the medical clinic.

"Those opposed?"

Noble's hand went up immediately, followed by Mrs. Chen, Jack Thompson, Maria Rodriguez, Old Pete, and the pharmacist - six opposing votes.

All eyes turned to Marcus, the bank's loan officer, who sat frozen in his chair. His face was pale, and his hands gripped the table's edge. "I..." he began, then stopped. "I don't know if

what I'm feeling is real anymore. What if Stanford's right?
What if I'm... compromised?"

"Marcus," Harold pressed gently. "Your vote?"

"I... I abstain." The words came out as barely a whisper.

Harold consulted his tablet again, scrolling through procedural
documents. "According to Cedar Springs Business Association bylaws, abstentions in tie votes default to approval of
motions addressing public safety." His voice carried no
triumph, only weary resignation. "The motion passes."

The silence that followed was deafening.

Mrs. Chen stood first, flour dust no longer sparkling but
settling like ash around her feet. "Then we're done here." She
walked toward the door, her steps heavy with disappointment.

One by one, Noble's supporters filed out. Jack Thompson
paused at the door, looking back at the board members who'd
remained seated. "Forty years I've been building things in this
town," he said quietly. "Never thought I'd see the day Cedar
Springs chose fear over possibility."

Stanford was already opening his briefcase, pulling out official forms. "I'll begin the preliminary assessment tomorrow
morning at eight. The process typically takes forty-eight
hours for a community this size."

Noble was the last to leave. At the doorway, he turned back to
face Harold. "You know what your father's printing press
could do," he said softly. "You've felt it yourself. When this is
over, and Stanford's protocols have flattened every dream in
this town, remember that you chose this."

The door closed behind him with a sound like finality.

Harold remained seated as the other supporters of the motion quietly gathered their things. Dr. Martinez lingered. "Harold," she said hesitantly, "in my practice lately, I've been seeing things... people healing faster than they should. Illnesses responding to treatments that shouldn't work. What if we're making a mistake?"

"What if we're not?" Harold replied, but his voice lacked conviction.

Through the tall windows of the Grand Hotel's meeting room, Cedar Springs spread below them in the gathering dusk. To Harold and the remaining board members, the town looked fragile, infected with dangerous anomalies that pulsed like fever through familiar streets. Shadows moved wrong. Light bent in impossible ways. The very air seemed contaminated with dreams.

But outside on the hotel steps, Noble and his supporters saw the same view in a different light. Cedar Springs glowed with awakening possibility. Each street corner held stories waiting to be told. Every storefront promised transformation. The evening air hummed with potential that had finally found its voice.

Marcus emerged from the hotel alone, strolling past both groups without speaking to either. At the bottom of the steps, he stopped and looked up at the clouds in the sky. Tomorrow, Stanford Blackwell would begin his assessment. Within forty-eight hours, federal oversight would be recommended or rejected based on his findings.

The town that had awakened together six weeks ago now stood divided, each half convinced they were saving Cedar Springs from the other.

In his room, Stanford drafted his preliminary report: "Community exhibits classic signs of magical emergence with significant population resistance to normalization protocols. Federal intervention is strongly recommended to prevent complete social collapse."

He scheduled the message to send at dawn, when Diana Wells would be preparing for her flight to Massachusetts.

Cedar Springs slept fitfully that night, caught between dreams of what it was becoming and nightmares of what it might lose.

10

DIVIDED GROUND

The morning after the vote, Cedar Springs felt fractured. Noble unlocked Manning's Hardware at dawn, the keys at his chest humming with nervous energy. Through the windows, he watched Harold's supporters hurry past without looking in. Their footsteps sounded hollow on the sidewalk.

Mrs. Chen arrived first, her apron still dusted with flour from the predawn baking. "My bread," she said, her voice tight with worry. "Something's wrong. The loaves are burning even when the oven temperature stays steady."

Jack Thompson stepped in, sawdust clinging to his shirt. "My workshop," he said softly. "The wood keeps splintering. Forty years of experience, and suddenly I'm making mistakes like a rookie."

One by one, Noble's supporters gathered. Each brought stories of gifts faltering, magic flickering like candles in the wind. The town's division was poisoning their awakening from within.

"The flowers," Maria said, holding wilted blooms. "They're losing their colors. Customers are complaining that the arrangements look ordinary."

Sarah raised her camera, then lowered it with frustration. "Half the shots are coming out blurred. Like the lens won't focus properly." Noble felt both keys pulse with alarm. The doubt Harold's faction carried was spreading through Cedar Springs like an infection. Fear was strangling the magic they'd fought to protect.

Jenny opened Rosa's ledger, its pages flickering between story and blank parchment. "Gran wrote about this," she said, her voice strained. "When communities split, the magic turns unstable. Feeds on conflict."

Through the front windows, they watched Stanford Blackwell emerge from the Grand Hotel with official-looking equipment. He moved systematically from business to business, documenting every flicker of instability.

"He's building his case," Noble said grimly. "Every burned loaf, every splintered board proves his point about dangerous anomalies." Mrs. Chen wrung her hands. "What if he's right? What if we're making people sick with memory-bread?"

"What if Harold was protecting us all along?" Jack asked, staring at his bandaged fingers.

The gathering now felt desperate, not celebratory. Each person questioned their own experiences. The magic that had felt so certain yesterday wavered under the weight of communal doubt.

Noble tried to rally them. "Remember what you felt," he said. "Remember why your crafts came alive." But even as he spoke, the keys at his chest grew colder. Sarah's photographs showed only ordinary tools and shadows. Jenny's ledger displayed simple inventory lists. The very act of defending their gifts seemed to make them fade.

By afternoon, Stanford had filled three folders with documentation. Insurance complaints about Mrs. Chen's "contaminated" bread. Safety violations from Jack's workshop accidents. Customer reports of "hallucinogenic experiences" at various businesses. "Forty-seven documented incidents in eight hours," he announced to Harold's emergency committee. "Federal oversight protocols require immediate intervention."

Noble stood at his store windows, watching Cedar Springs tear itself apart. Half the town avoided Main Street entirely, afraid of magical contamination. The other half moved with frantic energy, trying to prove their gifts were real and safe.

The division was killing everything they'd awakened. At sunset, as Noble's supporters gathered for what felt like a final attempt to restore their magic, Sarah spotted the black sedan turning onto Main Street. Official government plates. Tinted windows. The kind of vehicle that carried federal authority.

"Someone's coming," she said quietly. The sedan stopped directly in front of Manning's Hardware. The engine cut off with mechanical precision. For a moment, nobody moved. Then the driver's door opened.

Diana Wells stepped onto Cedar Springs' sidewalk like judgment arriving ahead of schedule. Professional suit, briefcase, eyes that missed nothing. She surveyed the fractured town with the calm assessment of someone who'd performed this duty seventeen times before.

Noble felt both keys go silent against his chest. "Good evening," Diana said, her voice carrying across the sudden stillness. "I'm Diana Wells, Federal Oversight Commission. I believe you've been expecting me."

Stanford appeared at her side, folders ready. Harold emerged from the print shop, relief and regret warring on his face. The town's supporters and opponents faced each other across Main Street like armies preparing for a final battle.

Cedar Springs held its breath, caught between the magic struggling to survive and the authority determined to contain it. Diana opened her briefcase with practiced efficiency. "Mr. Manning," she said, looking directly at Noble through the store windows, "we need to talk."

Noble stepped outside, the keys at his chest cold as winter metal. Sarah, Jenny, and the others followed, forming a protective circle behind him. Across the street, Harold emerged with his supporters, their faces a mix of relief and uncertainty.

Diana studied the fractured gathering with clinical precision. "I'm Diana Wells, Federal Oversight Commission for Anomalous Activity Management. Based on Mr. Blackwell's preliminary assessment, Cedar Springs exhibits Category Four magical emergence with documented public safety violations."

She pulled documents from her briefcase. "Forty-seven incidents logged in the past eight hours. Food contamination causes hallucinogenic episodes. Workshop accidents involving experienced craftsmen. Insurance claims for property damage caused by..." she consulted her notes, "reality distortion fields."

Stanford stepped forward with his folders. "The pattern matches seventeen previous interventions. Community division, escalating incidents, institutional breakdown."

"What are you proposing?" Noble asked, though the keys' silence already told him the answer.

Diana's voice remained level. "Immediate implementation of the Stability Enhancement Protocol. All anomalous activities will be neutralized within seventy-two hours. Affected businesses will receive federal compensation for the modifications to their equipment. Residents experiencing persistent hallucinogenic symptoms will be relocated to appropriate treatment facilities."

Mrs. Chen gasped. "Treatment facilities?"

"Standard procedure," Diana replied. "Those deeply affected by magical exposure require professional care. The symptoms you're experiencing aren't real gifts, Mrs. Chen. They're neurological disruptions caused by proximity to unstable reality fields."

Jack stepped forward, his bandaged hand clenched. "Neurological disruptions? I've been working with wood for forty years. I know when something's different."

"Yes, Mr. Thompson. You've suffered three workplace injuries this week after forty years of safe practice. The anomalous activity is compromising your judgment and motor skills."

Diana turned to address Harold's group directly. "The business association made the correct decision. Federal oversight prevents these situations from deteriorating into complete social collapse."

Harold shifted uncomfortably. "We voted for preliminary safety protocols, not..." "Not what, Mr. Whitaker?" Diana's tone sharpened slightly. "Your preliminary protocols are insufficient. Mr. Blackwell documented seventeen separate violations this afternoon alone. Your printing press is producing text that moves independently on the page. That's not a preliminary safety issue. That's a reality breach requiring immediate containment."

Sarah raised her camera, but the viewfinder showed only static. "You're doing this," she said accusingly. "You're suppressing the magic just by being here."

Diana nodded. "Standard dampening field. It prevents escalation during intervention procedures. The symptoms you're experiencing – the fading abilities, the equipment failures – prove how unstable your situation had become."

Stanford opened another folder. "Without intervention, Millbrook, Vermont, followed this exact pattern. Three weeks later, six residents were hospitalized with psychotic breaks. Four businesses were destroyed. The town never recovered."

"But that's not what's happening here," Noble protested. The keys at his chest remained stubbornly silent. Isn't it?" Diana gestured toward the divided crowd. "Half your community requested federal protection. The other half is experiencing collective hallucinations. Your magical emergence has fractured social cohesion and endangered public safety. These are textbook indicators for immediate intervention.

Jenny clutched Rosa's ledger, its pages now showing only blank parchment. "My grandmother wrote about federal agents," she said desperately. "About people who came to stop the magic before."

"Your grandmother's writings are part of the documented evidence," Stanford said gently. "Generational delusions often accompany magical emergence. The ledger you believe contains your grandmother's words is blank, Jenny. It has always been blank."

The gathered supporters looked at each other with growing horror. Their gifts were fading not from doubt, but from Diana's presence. The dampening field was erasing everything they'd discovered about themselves.

Diana consulted her tablet. "The mobile normalization unit arrives at 0600 tomorrow. All affected individuals will report for psychological evaluation. Businesses showing anomalous activity will be temporarily closed for equipment recalibration."

"And if we refuse?" Noble asked.

Diana's expression didn't change. "Refusal to cooperate with federal safety protocols constitutes willful endangerment of public welfare. Affected individuals would be transferred to secure treatment facilities until their conditions stabilize."

The ultimatum hung in the cooling evening air. Diana Wells had arrived not as a negotiator but as an executioner. The divided town had already signed its own death warrant.

11

WHEN ANCIENT
POWER MEETS FORCE

Diana opened her briefcase with practiced efficiency, withdrawing a thick folder of official documents. The federal seals gleamed like weapons in the afternoon light. Noble felt both keys go cold against his chest as she approached Manning's Hardware's entrance.

"By order of the Federal Emergency Management Authority," Diana announced, her voice carrying across Main Street, "this property is hereby designated a Class Four contamination site requiring immediate quarantine."

She handed Noble the court order, its letterhead sharp as judgment. "Effective immediately, all personnel are barred from entering the premises. The building will remain sealed pending completion of the normalization process."

Noble stared at the legal papers. Federal court stamps. Emergency health powers. Constitutional authority suspended under the Anomalous Activity Protection Act. Every line of bureaucratic text spelled the end of Manning's Hardware as he knew it.

"You're seizing my store?" he said, his voice barely steady.
"We're protecting the public," Diana corrected. "The energy readings from this location exceed safe exposure limits by four hundred percent. Continued operation would constitute willful endangerment."

Agent Martinez stepped forward with yellow tape and official seals. Within minutes, Manning's Hardware was wrapped like a crime scene, its doors marked with federal warnings about contaminated environments.

The townspeople gathered in horrified silence. Mrs. Chen clutched her basket of bread, now ordinary under the dampening field's influence. Jack Thompson's sawdust had lost its starlight. Even Harold's printing press sat silent, its magical words reduced to simple ink.

"How long?" Sarah asked, her camera hanging lifeless around her neck.

"Indefinitely," Diana replied, consulting her tablet. "Until our scientists determine the contamination has been fully neutralized. It could be months. Could be years."

Jenny approached the sealed entrance with Rosa's ledger, but the pages now showed only blank parchment. The stories, the wisdom, the generations of accumulated truth had vanished under federal oversight.

"The ledger," she whispered. "Gran's words. They're gone."

"The hallucinations are fading," Diana said with clinical satisfaction. "Your perceptions are returning to baseline normal. This proves the treatment is working."

Noble felt something fundamental break inside his chest where the keys had lived. The connection to his grandfather's legacy, to Eleanor's vision, to everything Cedar Springs had become, strained against federal authority.

Harold stepped forward, his face a mix of relief and uncertainty. "The business association supports this action," he said, but his voice lacked conviction. "Public safety must come first."

"Exactly," Diana agreed, making notes on her tablet. "Mr. Whitaker understands the necessity of intervention. Unlike others who've let emotional attachment cloud their judgment."

She gestured toward the processing station her agents had established in the town square. "All individuals showing contamination symptoms must report for medical evaluation. Those with advanced exposure will require extended treatment at specialized facilities."

The dampening field pulsed stronger, and Noble watched Cedar Springs forget itself in real time. Colors faded from Maria's flowers. Music died in the air around Harold's print shop. Even the morning light seemed to lose its capacity for wonder.

But Diana's instruments continued to show anomalous readings centered on Noble himself.

"Mr. Manning," she said, approaching him with her tablet extended, "you're still generating significant energy patterns. I need you to submit to immediate medical evaluation."

Noble looked at the readings on her screen. The numbers meant nothing to him, but he felt what they measured: the keys pulsing deeper in his chest, beyond the reach of her technology.

"The treatment won't work," he said quietly. "You've sealed the store, scattered the people, suppressed every visible sign of magic. But some transformations go deeper than buildings or businesses."

"Persistent contamination creates delusions of significance," Diana replied, but her voice carried less certainty than before. "The medical team will help you understand what's real."

"Will they help you understand?" Noble asked. Diana stepped back as if struck. Her instruments showed Noble's energy signature intensifying despite maximum dampening field strength. According to every protocol she'd learned, this was impossible.

"Agent Martinez," she ordered, "establish a containment perimeter around Subject One. Prepare for enhanced suppression protocols."

The federal agents moved to surround Noble, but he remained perfectly calm in the center of their circle. Through the sealed windows of Manning's Hardware, Sarah could see tools arranged precisely as her grandfather had placed them decades ago. The store waited, patient and unchanged, while bureaucracy decided its fate.

"You know what your equipment doesn't measure," Noble said to Diana. "The reason you became a federal agent. The pain that drives you to see danger in every awakening."

Diana's hand moved unconsciously to the locket at her throat. "My mother died because of magical contamination. I prevent other families from suffering the same loss."

"Your mother died because she had no support," Noble said. "No community to help her balance what she discovered. No foundation to build her transformation on."

"She died because bread carried psychoactive compounds that altered her brain chemistry," Diana snapped. "The autopsy showed cellular changes consistent with toxin exposure."

"Show me the full report," Noble said.

Diana hesitated. The complete autopsy file contained anomalies she'd never shared with her colleagues. Cellular structures that resembled crystal formations. Neural pathways that suggested enhanced connectivity rather than damage. Brain chemistry that indicated expanded perception rather than hallucination.

"The report is classified," she said.

"Because what you found scared you more than what you lost," Noble replied. Agent Martinez approached with restraint equipment. "Ma'am, should we proceed with containment?"

Diana stared at Noble, her training warring with doubts she'd buried for three years. Her instruments screamed warnings about energy levels that defied every model she'd studied. Manning's Hardware sat sealed but somehow still radiating power that her technology couldn't explain or suppress.

"Sir," she said to Noble, "you're coming with us for extended evaluation."

But as the agents moved to take him, Noble smiled with quiet certainty.

"Diana," he said, "when you examine the pocket binder in my jacket pocket, remember what your mother was really trying to tell you."

Diana looked down at the evidence bag containing Noble's personal effects. Among the items was a small 5x7 stack of photos, bound together with a simple white cover. She'd catalogued it, bagged it, but not examined. "What are these photos, Mr. Manning?"

"Those were taken by Eleanor, some of her last photographs," Noble said as the agents led him toward the federal transport vehicle. "The pictures she died taking. They show what your instruments can't measure and your protocols can't suppress."

As the van pulled away with Noble inside, Diana checked to make sure the bag of Noble Manning's personal effects was secure. She briefly wondered how these could be either proof of delusion or evidence of truth beyond her understanding.

Manning's Hardware remained sealed behind federal tape, but somehow Diana felt it watching her through its darkened windows.

12

—————

THE EVIDENCE OF TRUTH

Diana sat alone in her mobile command unit, the fluorescent lights casting harsh shadows across the evidence bag containing Noble Manning's personal effects. Standard protocol required cataloguing all items, but something made her hands tremble as she reached for the manila envelope tucked behind his driver's license.

Three black-and-white photographs, bound together with a simple rubber band and covered in white cardboard, fell onto the metal desk. The first showed a woman with a camera at the edge of Cedar Springs, but layers of light in the image suggested figures moving between dimensions, existing in spaces her equipment couldn't measure.

The second photograph made her catch her breath. The same photographer stood inside Manning's Hardware, tools casting shadows that told stories of their creations. But Diana's training kicked in - elaborate hoaxes were common in contamination cases. People desperate to validate their delusions often create false evidence.

Then she saw the third photograph.

158

Her mother's face stared back at her from a Vermont kitchen Diana had never seen documented. But this wasn't from any official case file. Margaret Wells stood holding bread that glowed with impossible light, her expression radiant with recognition rather than the confusion Diana remembered from those final weeks.

Diana's hands shook as she reached for the case file she'd carried for three years. She flipped past the official incident report to the evidence photographs taken by the investigating team. Photo after photo showed her mother in increasing states of distress - vacant stares, trembling hands, the progressive deterioration that had justified her psychiatric commitment.

But Eleanor's photograph showed something different. Her mother's eyes held clarity, not madness. Joy, not delusion. The expression of someone finally understanding truth rather than succumbing to fantasy.

Diana spread the official case photos beside Eleanor's image. Same kitchen. Same time period, based on her mother's clothing. But the official photos had been cropped - edited to remove the glowing bread, the impossible light, anything that might suggest the magical contamination was real rather than imagined.

Her secure phone buzzed, but Diana ignored it, grabbing her laptop to access the classified Vermont files. The original digital photographs loaded slowly on her screen, and there it was - metadata showing digital alteration. Brightness reduced. Contrast adjusted. Anomalous light sources were edited out of every official image.

The federal team had manufactured evidence of her mother's decline.

Diana's training in photo analysis revealed the scope of the deception. Her mother's "vacant stares" were actually moments of wonder digitally altered to appear empty. Her "trembling hands" had been reaching for light that existed in Eleanor's unedited photograph but was removed from official documentation.

The medical files told the same story once Diana looked with new eyes. Her mother's tissue samples did show crystalline structures - but the analysis had been labeled as "toxin damage" rather than "enhanced neural development." Brain chemistry indicating "expanded perception" had been reclassified as "hallucinogenic contamination."

Every piece of evidence supporting magical reality had been systematically edited, mislabeled, or buried in classified annexes that Diana had never been shown.

Her secure phone rang insistently. "Agent Wells, status report on Subject One."

Diana stared at Eleanor's photograph - the only unedited record of what her mother had actually experienced. Not a mental breakdown, but an awakening. Not contamination, but evolution.

"Agent Wells, respond immediately."

Diana now understood why the photograph would stop a federal agent in their tracks. For three years, she'd built her identity around preventing other families from experiencing what she thought was her mother's tragic descent into madness. But Eleanor's camera had captured the truth Diana's own agency had hidden from her.

Her mother hadn't been saved from magical contamination.

She'd been destroyed for evolving beyond the parameters someone else found unacceptable.

The woman Diana had spent years trying to avenge had never needed avenging in the first place.

The phone persisted in screaming for attention; she answered.

"Detained for enhanced evaluation," she replied automatically, her eyes fixed on her mother's image.

"Federal medical team reports unprecedented resistance to standard treatment. Recommend escalation to Level 7 protocols."

Level 7 meant psychosurgical intervention; brain modification to remove persistent magical contamination. Noble Manning would return to Cedar Springs as a docile shell, all traces of transformation erased.

"Understood," Diana said, ending the call.

But she stared at the photographs, her training warring with memories she'd buried. Her mother's final weeks in Vermont hadn't been random deterioration. Margaret had spoken of childhood memories awakening through her bread - specific details about Ireland that proved accurate when Diana later researched them. Her grandmother's recipes. Songs her mother had never learned but somehow knew. Stories of relatives who'd died before Margaret was born, yet whose lives she could describe with startling precision.

Diana had dismissed these as elaborate hallucinations. But what if they weren't?

She picked up the photos again, labeled: "Eleanor Manning's final shots. She died trying to show us what we were too scared to see. Margaret Wells wasn't alone that night at Miller's Bridge. She was seeking help, not following delusions. Your mother was awakening, not dying. She just had no one to teach her how."

Diana's hands trembled as she read the note twice, three times. How could Noble Manning know about Miller's Bridge? About her mother's final night? The details weren't in any public record.

She opened her laptop and accessed the classified Vermont files she'd helped compile. The incident report described Margaret Wells driving off Miller's Bridge alone, following directions whispered by contaminated bread. However, Diana had never reviewed the traffic camera footage from that night.

The digital files loaded slowly on her secure connection. Camera footage from Route 108, timestamped three hours before her mother's death. Diana watched Margaret's car approach Miller's Bridge, then stop. The image quality was poor, but the movement in the frame suggested that other figures were near the vehicle.

Margaret sat in her car for seventeen minutes. The timestamp showed her speaking, gesturing, as if conversing with someone. However, the thermal imaging revealed no other heat signatures or evidence of additional people.

Unless those people existed in spectrums Diana's equipment couldn't measure.

Yet the photograph showed what the traffic cameras had missed - figures of light surrounding the vehicle, not pushing Margaret toward destruction but reaching toward her with what looked like desperate attempts at guidance.

Diana's scientific training forced her to consider the evidence objectively. Three independent sources - Eleanor's photographs, Noble's note, and the traffic footage - suggested her mom, Margaret Wells, hadn't been alone during her final hours. Something had been trying to communicate with her, to help her understand what she was experiencing.

But Margaret had no support system, no community to help her integrate expanded perception. The isolation had killed her, not the magic.

Diana reached for her secure phone, then stopped. If she reported these findings, the photographs would likely be classified and disappear into files. Noble would undergo psychosurgical modification. Cedar Springs would be normalized according to protocol.

She looked at her mother's face in Eleanor's photograph, glowing with recognition rather than madness. Margaret Wells hadn't been poisoned by magical bread. She'd been awakening to something extraordinary without anyone to guide her safely through the transformation.

Diana made her choice.

She gathered Eleanor's photographs and her mother's complete file, sealing them in a waterproof envelope. Outside her command unit, fellow agents prepared equipment for departure, assuming the Cedar Springs case was closed.

She slipped away from the mobile base and found her rental car. The federal medical facility was four hours away. Noble Manning waited there for a treatment that would erase everything he'd become.

But Eleanor's photographs had shown Diana something her instruments couldn't measure, and her protocols were designed to destroy - evidence that some transformations were worth preserving, even at the cost of everything she'd built her career defending.

Diana pressed harder on the accelerator. She had until dawn to decide whether she was her mother's daughter or just another federal agent following orders that might be fundamentally wrong.

13

A TOWN DIVIDED

The morning after Noble's arrest, Cedar Springs woke to the acrid smell of fear. Sarah stood outside Manning's Hardware, breathing in the sharp scent of federal adhesive from the yellow tape that sealed her family's legacy. The metallic taste of desperation coated her tongue as she pressed her face against the window, watching dust motes settle on shelves where tools no longer hummed with purpose.

Jenny approached with Rosa's ledger clutched against her chest, but the leather binding felt cold beneath her fingertips. The pages rustled like autumn leaves when she opened them, revealing nothing but blank parchment where stories had once danced in flowing script. The dampening field's influence lingered, bitter as burnt coffee in the back of her throat.

"They took him," Sarah said, her voice cracking like glass in winter air. Through the sealed windows, she could see her father's coffee cup still sitting on the counter, a ring of brown stain on the wood grain. The sterile odor of federal efficiency had replaced the familiar aroma of his morning brew.

Mrs. Chen emerged from her bakery, the yeasty warmth that usually surrounded her now absent. Her hands, once dusted with flour that sparkled like stardust, were clean and ordinary. The bread she carried smelled like simple carbohydrates, nothing more. "My loaves," she whispered, breaking one open to reveal a plain white interior. "They don't remember anymore."

Jack Thompson shuffled down Main Street, sawdust clinging to his work shirt, but the particles no longer caught light like captured stars. His calloused palms felt rough and empty when he rubbed them together, the wood's songs silenced. Even the air around him smelled only of pine resin and turpentine, stripped of the forest mysteries his materials had once carried.

The federal command unit's diesel generator coughed black smoke into the morning sky, its mechanical rumble drowning out the subtle sounds of awakening that Cedar Springs had learned to treasure. Agent Martinez supervised the installation of monitoring equipment, her radio crackling with static that tasted sharp and electric on the tongue.

Harold Whitaker locked the print shop behind him, the keys jangling with mundane metal sounds. His fingers were stained with ordinary ink, nothing more than pigment and solvent. The printing press inside sat silent, its rollers clean of the magical words that had once made paper come alive with possibility.

The town's division became apparent in how people moved through space. Harold's faction walked purposefully toward normal routines, their footsteps crisp on concrete, breathing the fresh air of renewed rationality. They spoke in measured tones that lacked harmony, planning Cedar Springs' future based on practical considerations and established business models.

Sarah's group moved like mourners, their steps soft and hesitant, hands reaching for magic that no longer responded to their touch. They whispered to each other with voices hoarse from grief, tasting salt tears and the metallic aftertaste of loss. The air around them felt thin, as if something essential had been drained from the atmosphere.

Stanford Blackwell's sedan pulled into Main Street as the afternoon shadows grew long. Sarah felt her pulse quicken as she recognized the man whose protocols had seemingly destroyed everything they'd built. But when he stepped from the vehicle, his movements seemed different, less rigid than she remembered.

His suit jacket hung loose, as if he'd lost weight or perhaps shed some burden. When he approached the sealed hardware store, his breathing came in shallow gasps that carried the scent of regret mixed with something else - coffee and old paper, like a library long closed.

Jenny looked up from Rosa's empty ledger, her grief transforming into anger as hot as summer pavement. "You did this," she said, her voice sharp enough to cut glass. "Your protocols. Your fear. You destroyed what we built."

Stanford's hands trembled as he reached toward the federal tape, then pulled back. "The normalization wasn't supposed to happen this quickly. Diana Wells moved faster than expected."

"Don't blame her," Jenny said, clutching the blank ledger to her chest. The leather binding creaked with the sound of old doors closing. "This is what you wanted. This is what you've done to seventeen other towns."

Stanford's perfect composure cracked like ice in spring. "You don't understand the risks involved. I've seen what happens when magical emergence goes unchecked."

"Have you?" Jenny's voice carried Rosa's accent, strengthened by fury. "Or have you seen what happens when magic has no foundation to build on? No community to support it? No wisdom to guide it?"

The air around them grew thick with tension, tasting of copper and the coming storms. Sarah raised her camera, capturing Stanford's reflection in the sealed windows of Manning's Hardware - a man haunted by the shadows of what he'd once been.

"Tell her about the bookstore," Sarah said quietly, lowering her camera. "Tell her about the books that whispered stories."

Stanford's face went white as fresh flour. "How do you..."

"Noble told us he looked you up before the meeting. It was all there. Everything." Jenny said, stepping closer. The scent of her grief mixed with something sharper - the smell of truth cutting through lies. "About the store you owned. The community center you designed. The people who lost their savings because you had magic but no wisdom to guide it."

Stanford's briefcase slipped from his fingers, landing on the pavement with a sound like breaking bones. Documents scattered in the autumn wind, protocols and procedures mixing with fallen leaves. "That was different. I was young, inexperienced."

"You were what we were six months ago," Jenny said, her voice softening like butter in warm sunlight. "Awakening to something wonderful without understanding how to balance it safely."

The air grew still around them. Mrs. Chen approached with her basket of ordinary bread; the simple yeast scent offered a pale echo of what her bakery had once provided. Even she could smell the change in Stanford - cologne giving way to the musty odor of old books, as if memory was awakening something long buried.

"The books," Jenny continued, kneeling to gather his scattered papers. Her fingers brushed his as she handed them back, and he flinched at the contact. "They whispered their stories even when closed. You learned to stop listening because nobody taught you how to listen safely."

Stanford's voice cracked like autumn branches. "People trusted me. Invested everything they had in my vision of a community center where lives could transform. When it failed..." He stopped, his throat working as if swallowing broken glass.

"When it failed, you decided magic was the problem," Sarah said, her camera capturing the moment his professional mask finally slipped. "Not the lack of support. Not the absence of guidance. Magic itself."

"Seventeen towns," Jenny whispered, her words carrying the weight of accumulated loss. "Seventeen communities that awakened and were destroyed because you convinced yourself wonder was dangerous instead of learning how to make it safe."

Stanford looked at Manning's Hardware through the federal tape, his reflection distorted in the sealed windows. "I built the protocols to prevent what happened to me from happening to others."

"You built walls," Mrs. Chen said gently, offering him a piece of ordinary bread. It smelled only of wheat and yeast, but something in her gesture carried the memory of nourishment. "Walls between people and their gifts. Between communities and their possibilities."

Stanford took the bread with shaking hands. When he bit into it, tears ran down his cheeks, tasting of salt and long-buried dreams. "The books," he whispered. "They used to sing to me. Before I taught myself that singing books were impossible."

"They weren't impossible," Jenny said, opening Rosa's blank ledger. As Stanford watched, words began to appear on the empty pages - faint at first, like morning mist, but growing stronger. "They were just waiting for someone who remembered how to listen."

Stanford stared at the writing appearing in the ledger, his eyes wide with recognition and terror. "This shouldn't be happening. The dampening field should prevent..."

"Should prevent what?" Sarah asked, her camera clicking as it captured light returning to the world around Stanford. "Should prevent you from remembering who you used to be before you learned to be afraid?"

The evening air carried new scents - the musty sweetness of old paper and binding glue, stories long untold. Stanford's rigid posture softened as something he'd buried for decades began to surface. His breathing deepened, drawing in the possibility that wonder might not always lead to destruction.

"Cedar Springs was different," he said finally, his voice thick with understanding. "You had Noble. You had the hardware store's foundation. You had each other." He looked around at the small group of supporters, their faces reflecting hope despite their loss. "I had none of that. When my store failed, I failed alone."

Jenny closed the ledger gently, but its pages continued to glow with returning stories. "You don't have to fail alone anymore," she said. "Diana Wells has the evidence. If she understands what Eleanor's photographs show, she might reverse the containment orders."

"And if she doesn't?" Sarah asked.

Stanford picked up his scattered papers, but his movements had changed. Less mechanical now, more human. "Then I spend whatever time I have left undoing what I've done. Starting with teaching the other sixteen towns how to remember what they lost."

The evening air carried the sounds of a community trying to remember how to breathe. But underneath the hollow footsteps and flattened conversations, something stirred - the faint whisper of stories attempting to return, of books remembering how to sing, of a man who had spent years running from magic finally turning to face what he'd lost.

14

AGAINST ORDERS

Diana's headlights cut through the darkness as she drove toward the federal medical facility, Eleanor's photographs spread across the passenger seat like tarot cards predicting an uncertain future. The dashboard clock read 2:47 AM. Level 7 psychosurgical protocols would begin at dawn, leaving her less than four hours to decide Noble Manning's fate.

The photographs seemed to pulse in the green light of her instrument panel. Her mother's face looked back at her from Eleanor's final shot, not confused or delusional but radiant with recognition. The taste of coffee had long since faded from Diana's mouth, replaced by the metallic flavor of adrenaline and the bitter aftertaste of three years spent following the wrong path.

Her secure phone buzzed against the leather seat. "Agent Wells, confirm your location." Diana's hands tightened on the steering wheel, knuckles white in the dashboard glow. "En route to facility for final case documentation."

172

"Understood. Subject One prep begins in ninety minutes. Dr. Hendricks requests your presence for the pre-surgical briefing."

The line went dead. Diana pressed harder on the accelerator, the engine's hum rising to match her racing pulse. Through the windshield, rural Massachusetts stretched endlessly under a star-scattered sky. The air conditioning carried the sterile scent of the federal sedan, nothing like the warm complexity of Cedar Springs' awakened atmosphere.

At 3:15 AM, the facility's lights appeared on the horizon like a constellation fallen to earth. Diana felt her stomach clench as she recognized the compound where seventeen communities' worth of "contaminated" individuals had undergone treatment. How many had been like her mother?

How many had been seeking guidance rather than experiencing delusion?

The checkpoint guards waved her through with practiced efficiency. Security lights bathed the complex in harsh white illumination that tasted sharp and artificial on her tongue. Diana parked outside the medical wing, her hands trembling as she gathered Eleanor's photographs.

Dr. Hendricks met her at the entrance, his lab coat crisp as fresh snow and carrying the antiseptic smell of absolute certainty. "Agent Wells. Right on schedule. Subject One is prepped and ready for Level 7 intervention."

Diana followed him through corridors that hummed with fluorescent authority. The air here felt thick, pressing against her lungs like cotton soaked in disinfectant. Through reinforced windows, she glimpsed other patients in various stages of treatment - former shopkeepers, craftspeople, dreamers who had touched magic and been deemed dangerous to themselves and society.

"The Manning case presents unusual challenges," Dr. Hendricks continued, his voice echoing off sterile walls. "Energy readings remain elevated despite seventy-two hours of intensive suppression therapy. The subject appears to generate his own field, independent of external magical sources."

They stopped outside a viewing window. Noble Manning sat in a white room, perfectly still in his hospital gown. Monitoring equipment surrounded him like electronic vultures, their screens showing patterns Diana had never seen before. His vitals were stable, but the energy readings pulsed with rhythms that reminded her of heartbeats or breathing.

"Fascinating case study," Dr. Hendricks said, making notes on his tablet. "The neural pathways show permanent alteration. Standard suppression protocols have no effect. Level 7 intervention is our only option."

Diana pressed her face against the cool glass, watching Noble breathe. His eyes were closed, but something about his posture suggested meditation rather than defeat. The harsh facility lighting couldn't quite drain the sense of depth that surrounded him, as if he existed in dimensions her instruments couldn't map.

"Show me his complete medical workup," Diana said.

Dr. Hendricks consulted his tablet, scrolling through data. "Blood chemistry shows trace compounds consistent with prolonged magical exposure. Brain scans reveal crystalline formations in neural tissue. Cellular analysis indicates structural changes at the molecular level."

Diana's breath caught. The crystalline formations were identical to what they'd found in her mother's autopsy. "Are the changes... degenerative?"

"Quite the opposite," Dr. Hendricks said, his voice carrying clinical fascination. "The subject's cognitive function tests above baseline normal. Reaction times are enhanced. Pattern recognition shows significant improvement. The magical exposure appears to have optimized rather than damaged neural function."

"Then why the Level 7 intervention?"

Dr. Hendricks looked at her with surprise. "Because optimized neural function in the direction of magical sensitivity represents a threat to social stability. The subject cannot be reintegrated into normal society while maintaining these enhancements."

Diana stared through the window at Noble, understanding flooding through her like ice water. The federal protocols weren't designed to heal magical contamination. They were designed to prevent human evolution beyond controllable parameters.

"I need to see the comparative data," she said. "All seventeen previous cases."

"That information is classified above your clearance level."

"I'm the primary investigating agent on this case. I have the authority to review all relevant medical data."

Dr. Hendricks hesitated, then led her to his office. The files loaded slowly on his secure terminal, years of documentation from normalized communities. Diana read with growing horror as the pattern began to emerge.

Every subject showed similar neural enhancements. Enhanced pattern recognition. Improved cognitive function. Expanded sensory perception. The medical evidence consistently indicated evolution rather than contamination.

But every subject had been returned to their communities as docile shells, their enhanced capabilities erased through psychosurgical intervention.

"My God," Diana whispered. "We've been lobotomizing people for developing beyond baseline human parameters."

"We've been maintaining social stability," Dr. Hendricks corrected. "Imagine the chaos if enhanced humans were allowed to integrate into normal populations. The inequality. The social disruption. The fear."

Diana pulled Eleanor's photographs from her briefcase and spread them across Dr. Hendricks' desk. Under the office's harsh lighting, the images seemed to glow with their own inner illumination. "Look at these. Really look."

Dr. Hendricks examined the photographs with clinical detachment, but Diana watched his expression change as he processed what he was seeing. The tool shadows telling stories. Margaret Wells' face was radiant with recognition - the figures of light at Miller's Bridge.

"Elaborate hallucinations," he said finally. "Consistent with advanced magical contamination."

"Or documentation of expanded reality perception," Diana countered. "What if our subjects aren't hallucinating? What if they're seeing aspects of reality that we've trained ourselves to ignore?"

Dr. Hendricks stepped back from the photographs. "Agent Wells, I recommend you submit to a psychological evaluation. Prolonged exposure to contaminated subjects can induce empathy syndrome."

Diana felt the weight of her choice settling around her like a shroud. She could submit to evaluation, allow Noble's treatment to proceed, and return to Cedar Springs to oversee its complete normalization. Safe. Predictable. Following orders.

Or she could trust Eleanor's photographs and her mother's memory. Trust that human consciousness was evolving rather than degenerating. Trust that magic wasn't contamination but expansion.

"I'm removing Subject One from the facility," she said.

"You don't have that authority."

Diana pulled out her federal credentials and her sidearm. "I'm Agent Diana Wells, Federal Oversight Commission. I'm declaring this subject critical to ongoing investigation. Any interference will be considered obstruction of federal operations."

Dr. Hendricks reached for his phone, but Diana's weapon remained steady. "The facility is under federal lockdown until I complete my assessment. No one enters or leaves without my authorization."

She backed toward the door; Eleanor's photographs clutched in her free hand. "Prep Subject One for immediate transport. We're returning to Cedar Springs."

"This is career suicide, Agent Wells."

Diana paused at the threshold, tasting the antiseptic air one last time. "No, Doctor. This is finally learning the difference between healing and harm."

At 4:33 AM, Diana helped Noble Manning into her sedan, his hospital gown replaced by civilian clothes that smelled of federal laundry detergent. He moved slowly, yet with quiet dignity, as if awakening from a deep sleep.

"Eleanor's photographs," he said as she started the engine. "You saw them."

"They showed me what I spent three years refusing to see." Diana pulled away from the facility, its lights shrinking in her rearview mirror. "My mother wasn't contaminated. She was evolving."

Noble settled into the passenger seat, breathing deeply of the night air flowing through the open windows. "The question now is whether Cedar Springs will be allowed to continue evolving or whether federal forces will stop us permanently."

Diana's phone buzzed with urgent messages - facility breach alerts, federal manhunt protocols, career-ending consequences. She turned off the device and drove toward the sunrise, carrying Cedar Springs' future in the space between duty and truth.

"We have three hours before they realize you're gone," she said. "Three hours to prove that magic and measurement can coexist safely."

Noble smiled, feeling the keys pulse warm against his chest despite everything the federal facility had tried to suppress. "Then we'd better make them count."

As they drove through the morning, Diana tasted possibility on her tongue for the first time in three years. Behind them, the federal facility scrambled to contain a breach that would either destroy the normalization program or prove that some transformations were worth the risk of embracing the unknown.

15

THE CLEANSING POWER OF LIGHT

Dawn painted Cedar Springs in shades of amber and possibility as Diana's sedan pulled onto Main Street. The federal tape still sealed Manning's Hardware, but something had changed in the town's breathing.

The air carried the scent of Mrs. Chen's bread baking despite the early hour, and the morning light seemed to bend around corners with deliberate purpose.

Noble stepped from the car. His bare feet touched familiar pavement like a sailor reaching home shore after years at sea. The keys on his chest pulsed with recognition. Warmth spread through his body like honey mixed with starlight. He tasted the town's awakening on his tongue. Yeast and sawdust, printer's ink and morning dew, layered with the metallic tang of fear, giving way to hope.

Sarah emerged from shadows between buildings. Her camera swayed against her chest as she ran. Morning light caught tears streaming down her face. Each drop carried years of patient waiting, of loving someone who refused to see what she saw. Noble caught her in his arms, still imbued with an antiseptic smell from the federal facility. Underneath pulsed the deeper scent of home and transformation.

Her camera hung around her neck. Eleanor's gift passed between generations. Her hands trembled too much to lift the device. For once, Sarah didn't need to capture the moment. She needed to live within its truth.

"They said you'd be different," Sarah whispered against his shoulder. She breathed in familiar warmth absent for so long. "Changed. Broken."

"I am changed," Noble replied. His voice carried new depths like a well finding underground rivers. "But not broken. Never broken."

Noble held his daughter by the shoulders. He looked directly into her eyes. In this moment, he saw their entire shared history. Every argument about what was real. Every time he'd dismissed her gifts. Every evening she'd spent alone with her camera while he buried himself in ledgers and measurements. The keys on his chest sang with the harmony of truth finally acknowledged.

A single tear traced down his weathered cheek. Morning light caught the drop like liquid silver. "Sarah, I need to say something I should have said years ago." His voice broke like ice in spring. "I drove you away when you needed me most. You were seeing truth with your mother's eyes. I was so afraid of what your vision might mean. I chose blindness over wonder."

Air around them shimmered with something beyond ordinary light. Forgiveness took visible form. Love found its voice after years of silence.

"You evolved so quickly. Bloomed like your mother before you. Instead of celebrating your gifts, I tried to contain them. I was terrified of acknowledging what you saw, what Eleanor saw. I'd have to admit I was failing everyone who counted on me to keep things steady." His hands shook as they touched her face. "I stole part of your childhood, didn't I? Made you grow up too fast. Forced you to choose between your gifts and your father."

Sarah's tears flowed freely now. Each one carried away years of hurt. The camera around her neck began warming. Eleanor's spirit stirred within old metal and glass.

"Dad, watching you suffer nearly broke me, that's why I had to move away," Sarah said. Her voice carried emotion but stayed clear with understanding. "But I had faith. Mom taught me this faith. Someday, you would see what we all saw. What we knew was as real as breathing. I couldn't force you to see any more than you could force yourself. The awakening had to come from within."

She reached up to touch the tear on his cheek. Where her finger met his skin, tiny sparks of light danced between them. The magic had always connected them… and finally acknowledged.

"Mom tried to show you gently. When she realized the time wasn't right, she waited. We all waited because we loved you too much to give up on you." Sarah's smile carried sunlight and starshine. "And now, Dad, we're so proud of you. Finally acknowledging what's as real as your ledgers but infinitely more important because this is life itself. The reason we build, measure, and keep records in the first place. To serve something larger than ourselves."

Morning air around them began singing with harmonics only they heard. Father and daughter finally seeing each other clearly. The wall of fear separating them dissolved like mist before dawn.

Jenny approached with Rosa's ledger. Its pages no longer blank but flickering with words appearing and fading like Aurora Borealis across night sky. The leather binding pulsed with warmth in her hands. Alive with accumulated stories of families healing, of love patient enough to wait for fear to transform into courage.

"The dampening field," she said softly. She watched magical light dance between Noble and Sarah. "Not weakening. Learning some connections are too strong to suppress."

Diana surveyed the gathering crowd with professional eyes that now saw beyond surface readings. Mrs. Chen hurried from her bakery, flour dusting her apron with light that sparkled like captured stars. Jack Thompson emerged from his workshop, sawdust clinging to his hair in patterns that resembled constellations. Even Harold approached from the print shop, ink staining his fingers with shadows that moved independently of the morning light.

"The federal response team will arrive within the hour," Diana announced, her voice carrying the authority of someone who had walked through fire and chosen her own burning. "They'll declare this an active containment breach. Full military protocols."

Noble approached Manning's Hardware's sealed entrance, his hands pressed against the yellow tape that tasted bitter as old medicine. Through the windows, he could see tools arranged exactly as his grandfather had left them, waiting with the patience of objects that understood their purpose transcended simple function.

"This building is more than a hardware store. It's a type of cathedral, a safe place for those open to the unseen world, to allow truth to follow them home," he said, feeling the keys pulse with certainty. "It teaches us that we are much more than meets the eye. By allowing it freely, it will strengthen rather than destabilize."

Diana's phone buzzed with urgent messages she no longer answered. Through the device's speaker came the distant sound of helicopters approaching, their rotors chopping the morning air like mechanical thunder. "They're coming faster than expected," she said. "We have minutes, not an hour."

Jenny opened Rosa's ledger fully, and stories poured from its pages like water from a broken dam. Words in multiple languages, some she recognized as her grandmother's Spanish, others ancient beyond naming. The scent of memory rose from the paper: cooking spices, woodsmoke, the salt air of oceans crossed by desperate hope.

"Gran wrote about this moment," Jenny said, her voice carrying Rosa's accent strengthened by recognition. "When the crossroads would be tested. When wonder would have to prove itself worthy of trust."

The helicopters grew louder, their approach vibrating through the soles of everyone's feet. Diana could taste military efficiency on the wind: jet fuel and tactical certainty, the metallic flavor of decisions made by committees who measured only what they feared to lose.

"They'll seal the entire downtown," she warned. "Establish a perimeter. Anyone showing magical contamination will be detained for indefinite treatment."

Mrs. Chen stepped forward, her basket of fresh bread releasing steam that carried the scent of more than flour and yeast. Each loaf held memories of comfort, healing, and the taste of home for those who had forgotten they belonged anywhere.

"Then we show them what contamination really looks like," she said, breaking open a roll that glowed with inner warmth.

Jack Thompson approached with a piece of wood that hummed with forest songs, its grain revealing patterns that spoke of growth rings counted in centuries, of storms weathered and seasons survived. "My grandfather taught me to read the wood's story," he said. "But I forgot how to listen until Cedar Springs remembered its own."

One by one, the townspeople stepped forward with their awakened crafts. Maria Rodriguez carried flowers that bloomed in colors beyond the ordinary spectrum, their fragrance opening doorways in the heart to rooms people forgot they had. Harold held pages fresh from his press, words that moved on the paper like living things, rearranging themselves to tell each reader exactly what they needed to understand.

The helicopters circled overhead, their downwash stirring dust that sparkled with possibility. Through the artificial wind, Noble felt the town's magic rising like morning mist, not chaotic or destructive but purposeful as sunrise.

"This is what they fear," he called over the rotor noise. "Not that magic will destroy communities, but that communities will discover they never needed to be controlled in the first place."

Diana watched the federal response team rappel from the helicopters, their black uniforms stark against Cedar Springs'

golden morning light. She recognized the commander -
Colonel Matthews, a man who measured success in problems
eliminated rather than solutions created. His boots hit the
pavement with mechanical precision, and immediately, the air
around him began to taste of suppression and control.

"Agent Wells," Colonel Matthews' voice cut through his tactical
headset's electronic crackle. "Step away from the contaminated
subjects. You're exhibiting signs of empathy syndrome."

Diana moved to stand beside Noble instead, Eleanor's
photographs clutched in her hands. "I'm exhibiting signs of
finally understanding what we've been destroying."

The tactical team deployed their equipment with practiced
efficiency - reality dampeners that hummed with electronic
authority, containment fields that pressed against the skin like
invisible walls, sensors that reduced wonder to numbers on
glowing screens.

But something unexpected happened as the dampening fields
activated. Instead of suppressing Cedar Springs' magic, the
federal equipment began to resonate with it. The electronic
hum shifted into harmonics that matched the town's awakened rhythm. Readouts flickered between normal parameters
and patterns the instruments weren't designed to measure.

"Equipment malfunction," one technician reported, his voice
tight with confusion. "Energy readings are off the charts, but
they're stable. Coherent. The subjects aren't generating chaos
- they're generating order."

Colonel Matthews examined his instruments with growing
frustration. Every protocol indicated the contaminated
subjects should collapse into psychotic episodes when
exposed to military-grade suppression. Instead, they stood

together with quiet dignity, their gifts brightening rather than fading under pressure.

"Increase suppression to maximum levels," he ordered.

The dampening fields intensified until the air itself seemed to thicken with electronic interference. Birds fell silent. Car engines stuttered. Even the morning light seemed pressed thin by artificial constraints.

But Noble stepped forward, the keys on his chest pulsing with rhythm older than fear. Around him, Cedar Springs' magic didn't fight the suppression - it embraced it, showing how wonder and control could dance together rather than destroy each other.

Mrs. Chen's bread continued to carry memories, but now those memories included the comfort of safety alongside adventure. Jack Thompson's wood sang forest songs, but harmonized with the steady rhythm of human heartbeats. Harold's words moved on the page, but spelled out practical truths alongside poetic mysteries.

"Impossible," Colonel Matthews whispered, staring at readings that showed magical activity strengthening under maximum suppression rather than weakening.

Diana approached with a thick folder. "My personal feelings don't override national security protocols," Matthews said, stepping back. "Equipment anomalies don't invalidate established procedures."

"Then look at this as a professional," Diana said, spreading neurological scans across his command vehicle's hood. "Medical files from all seventeen normalized communities. Enhanced neural connectivity, improved cognitive function, expanded sensory perception. We weren't curing damage - we were creating it."

Matthews examined the brain scans with growing unease. "These documents could be fabricated to support your compromised position."

"Check the metadata yourself," Diana challenged. She handed him a thumb drive with everything in one place. His secure tablet confirmed authenticity. Page after page contradicted his briefings. Medical reports describing evolution rather than contamination. Psychological evaluations show enhanced empathy rather than delusion.

"Even if these raise questions," Matthews said slowly, "I have orders from people with broader strategic perspectives."

The sound of approaching vehicles interrupted his resistance. Three news vans rounded the corner onto Main Street, satellite dishes gleaming in the morning light. Behind them came more vehicles - reporters, camera crews, equipment trucks, creating a convoy of media attention.

"Sir," one of Matthews' tactical team members reported, "we have civilian media on site. Multiple networks are setting up broadcast positions."

Matthews stared at the news crews with alarm. Federal operations were classified. "How did they…"

"Someone wanted the world to see this," Diana said.

The lead reporter approached with her microphone. "This is Janet Morrison, Channel 7 News, reporting live from Cedar Springs, Massachusetts, where federal agents have surrounded what appears to be an extraordinary situation involving the same agency responsible for operations in seventeen other communities."

Colonel Matthews felt his radio crackle with urgent commands. "Matthews, implement news blackout immediately." Matthews looked around. It was too late; his soldiers were fully engaged in the operation to mount an evacuation, especially now.

But cameras were already broadcasting live streams of Cedar Springs' awakened residents, their gifts visible to millions of viewers.

A white sedan pulled to the perimeter. Stanford Blackwell stepped out, his suit wrinkled but his bearing carrying new purpose.

"Blackwell!" Matthews called with relief, having worked with him on seventeen other assignments. "Agent Wells has been compromised. I need you to restore order."

Stanford approached. "Hello, Robert. You look exactly like your father did in that uniform."

Matthews stiffened. "That's Colonel Matthews, Blackwell. Maintain professional protocol."

"Professional protocol," Stanford repeated bitterly. "Like the protocol your father, Major Matthews, used when he discovered his wife could make flowers bloom out of season? When eight-year-old Bobbie came home crying because kids called his mother a witch?"

The colonel's hand moved toward his sidearm. "My family history isn't relevant to this operation."

"I remember the Fort Carson reports, Robert, how your father had your mother undergo psychiatric evaluation. Six months in military psychiatric care until she learned to stop making impossible things happen."

Matthews' tactical visor reflected morning light, but Stanford could see the boy who'd watched his family destroyed by fear of the extraordinary. "She got better," Matthews said, voice cracking.

"She got broken," Stanford corrected gently. "Just like seventeen communities got broken when we convinced ourselves safety mattered more than wonder. Your mother wasn't sick - she had magic. Instead of learning to support her gifts safely, your father chose to have them surgically removed from her mind. She came home empty."

Mrs. Chen approached the tactical perimeter with fresh bread. "Your soldiers look hungry. Such a long morning."

Despite orders to maintain distance, one young corporal accepted a roll. The moment he bit into it, tears began flowing as he tasted memories of his grandmother's kitchen, unconditional love, and belonging.

"Martinez," he whispered, "it tastes like home. Like when my abuela made pan dulce before she died."

Another soldier, then another, experienced the same healing. News cameras captured hardened federal agents weeping as they remembered their humanity.

"Sir," Sergeant Rodriguez reported, eyes wet, "the subjects aren't harming anyone. They're helping us remember things we'd forgotten."

Diana approached Matthews with another thick file. "Testimonies from Fort Carson military families. Eighteen documented cases. Spouses, children, parents - all showing enhanced abilities, all subjected to psychiatric intervention, all returned as shells."

He opened the folder with trembling hands. Name after name of military families destroyed by the same protocols he now enforced.

"This represents systematic suppression," Diana said quietly. "Military dependents showing enhanced abilities disappear into psychiatric facilities. Records get altered. Families are told their loved ones suffered breakdowns rather than break-throughs."

A child's voice cut through his resistance. Sofia Rodriguez approached, carrying a crayon drawing that produced impossible colors.

"Mister soldier," she called, holding up her picture, "this is your mama when she was happy."

The drawing showed a woman surrounded by flowers, face radiant with joy. But the sketch captured his mother's features with precision no six-year-old should possess - showing her before treatment destroyed her gifts.

"How do you know what my mother looked like?" Matthews whispered.

"She showed me. She wants you to know she forgives you for not being able to save her. You were just a little boy then, and little boys can't fight the whole army."

Forty years of suppressed grief broke through military discipline as cameras recorded everything. Matthews dropped to his knees, recognizing that his life's work had systematically destroyed people like his own mother.

"All teams, stand down," he ordered, voice breaking. "Command, this is Matthews. The Cedar Springs operation has revealed critical flaws in our normalization protocols. These people aren't contaminated - they're evolved. I'm requesting an immediate halt to all interventions."

"Negative, Colonel. You have your orders. Proceed with containment."

Matthews removed his radio and placed it where cameras could film its continued transmission. "Forty years of service," he said while millions watched, "and I'm throwing it away because a child's drawing made my soldiers remember they're human."

The news reporter stepped closer. "Colonel, are you saying your mother was subjected to the same protocols?"

Matthews looked directly into the camera. "My mother had magic. We destroyed her for being more than we understood. We've been destroying people for decades, calling evolution contamination."

His radio crackled from the pavement: "Colonel Matthews, you are relieved of command. Return to base for psychological evaluation."

"Some orders," he said to Stanford, "are too small for what we're becoming."

16

THE TEACHING BEGINS

The news crews packed their equipment as afternoon sunlight painted Main Street in colors the cameras couldn't capture. Cedar Springs hummed with a frequency deeper than electronic interference, the sound of a community breathing together after holding its breath for days.

Noble stood before Manning's Hardware as federal agents removed the yellow tape, each strand peeling away with the sticky sound of barriers dissolving.

Sarah raised her camera but lowered it without taking the shot. Her father's hands trembled as he unlocked the door, which his grandfather had first opened over a century ago. Noble paused briefly and smiled as he recognized the familiar scents, having spent the last 60 years of his life watching, learning, and evolving. Now the delicious smell of dust, oil, and stories settled back into familiar corners.

Inside, the tools arranged themselves with quiet purpose. Hammers found their proper weight. Saws remembered their

193

voices. Even the old register hummed with satisfaction as Noble ran his first transaction since the federal siege, selling Mrs. Chen a box of nails while her bread filled the store with the scent of possibility.

Jenny opened Rosa's ledger to find new words appearing in multiple scripts, languages flowing together like streams joining a river. "People are coming," she read aloud, her grandmother's accent strengthening with recognition. "From places awakening like morning flowers. They need what Cedar Springs learned."

The first visitors arrived before the ink on Jenny's translation had dried. A family from Portland drove through the evening, their car windows down to breathe the air everyone was talking about. The mother carried a wooden box carved by her grandfather, which had started singing old songs three weeks ago. Her teenage daughter sketched pictures with charcoal sticks, drawings moving on paper like living memories.

"We saw the news," the mother explained, her voice rough with a mix of hope and exhaustion. "The interviews with Colonel Matthews. Agent Wells and those horrible protocols. We thought we were going crazy until we watched your story."

Noble led them through Manning's Hardware while the store demonstrated its teaching. Tools revealed their purposes to be beyond simple function. Paint cans revealed colors existing between ordinary shades. Lumber whispered of forests and futures; homes built on foundations strong enough to support wonder.

Others followed the Portland family. A baker from Seattle whose sourdough starter had begun fermenting memories instead of flour. A mechanic from Eugene whose garage tools repaired more than engines, fixing relationships between drivers and their deepest dreams. An accountant from Boise whose spreadsheets calculated possibilities alongside profits.

Each arrival brought stories of awakening gifts struggling without support, communities dividing between those who embraced transformation and those who feared change. Cedar Springs became their classroom, demonstrating how wonder and wisdom could coexist harmoniously instead of competing for dominance.

Diana Wells established a temporary office at the Grand Hotel, processing requests from seventeen communities that were ready to reverse their normalization protocols. Her phone rang constantly with calls from mayors, business leaders, and federal agents questioning orders they'd followed without understanding their actual cost.

"The medical evidence was always there," she explained to a reporter from the Boston Globe, her voice carrying the authority of someone who had walked through fire and chosen truth over comfort. "Enhanced cognitive function. Improved pattern recognition. Expanded sensory perception. We called evolution contamination because someone up the chain benefits from keeping people afraid of their own potential."

Stanford Blackwell reopened his bookstore in the building adjacent to Manning's Hardware. The books whispered their stories again, pages turning themselves to reveal passages readers needed most. Children gathered for story hours, where tales came alive, as characters stepped from printed pages to act out adventures in three dimensions.

"Reading," Stanford told a group of librarians visiting from Colorado Springs, "was always about more than consuming information. Books want to transform readers, to plant seeds of possibility in minds ready to grow beyond their current boundaries."

Colonel Matthews faced a military tribunal but retained public support after his televised confession about federal overreach. Veterans' organizations rallied around his decision to choose human evolution over institutional control. His testimony about his mother's destruction sparked congressional hearings into decades of suppression protocols.

Harold Whitaker's printing press produced the first Cedar Springs Community Guide, words rearranging themselves to address each reader's specific needs. Business owners from across the region ordered copies, seeking practical advice for integrating magical emergence with regulatory compliance.

"Balance," Harold explained to a chamber of commerce delegation, his fingers stained with ink moving like living calligraphy, "comes from understanding regulatory frameworks exist to serve communities, not control them. When magic makes businesses more efficient, more profitable, more beneficial to customers, regulations should adapt rather than suppress."

Mrs. Chen expanded her bakery to accommodate cooking classes for visitors whose kitchens had begun producing impossible meals. Jack Thompson's workshop hosted carpentry seminars where wood taught apprentices to listen before cutting, to understand grain patterns as maps of possibility.

Maria Rodriguez established a garden center specializing in flowers that bloom beyond ordinary spectrums, their colors healing emotional wounds that conventional therapy couldn't reach. Her greenhouse became a pilgrimage destination for artists seeking pigments existing between imagination and reality.

The federal facility where Noble had been detained closed permanently after a congressional investigation revealed systematic human rights violations and evidence of Big Pharma exerting control over key executives. Dr. Hendricks testified about pressure from unnamed superiors to suppress cognitive enhancement rather than study its beneficial applications.

Through it all, Manning's Hardware served as the crossroads where visitors found tools for their own transformations. Noble measured nails and lumber while teaching customers to measure dreams alongside dimensions, to calculate wonder into their building plans.

Sarah documented the transformation with photographs that captured layers of reality, allowing visitors to learn to see them. Her images appeared in magazines worldwide, showcasing communities where magic and mundane life strengthened each other, rather than competing for dominance.

The evening brought the community together for the first Cedar Springs Magic Council, where elected representatives from awakened businesses met to establish protocols that protect both transformation and stability. Their discussions filled the air with the scent of democracy functioning as intended, citizens governing themselves rather than being ruled by distant fear.

"We're writing the manual," Jenny explained to a CNN reporter, Rosa's ledger open before her, as pages wrote themselves with collective wisdom.

"For communities ready to evolve beyond the limitations others tried to impose. The instructions were always here, waiting for people brave enough to read them."

The autumn air carried sounds of construction as Cedar Springs expanded to accommodate the growing stream of visitors. New businesses opened daily, each founded by awakened craftspeople seeking communities where their gifts could flourish without fear of federal intervention.

Noble stood on his front porch as darkness settled over the transformed town, feeling the keys pulse with completion in his chest. The journey from hardware store owner to guardian of transformation felt both endless and instantaneous, like all meaningful change.

Sarah joined him, her camera hanging silent around her neck. "Mom would have loved this," she said, breathing air thick with the scent of possibility realized.

"She's seeing it," Noble replied, watching lights flicker on throughout Cedar Springs, each window glowing with the warmth of people finally free to become who they were meant to be. "Through every photograph you take, every story you help tell. Eleanor's vision is living in everyone brave enough to choose growth over safety."

The evening star appeared above Manning's Hardware, its light bending around the building like recognition of a job well done. Cedar Springs had become what Noble's grandfather had envisioned when he first opened the store, what his father had protected through careful systems, and what Eleanor had captured in her final photographs.

A crossroads where people could safely traverse the space between what was and what could be, carrying tools for transformation back to communities ready to remember their own magic.

The phone inside Manning's Hardware rang with calls from distant towns reporting their own awakenings. Noble smiled, tasting tomorrow's possibilities on the autumn wind. The real work was beginning.

EPILOGUE

Ten years after Cedar Springs proved transformation and stability could coexist, twelve-year-old Emma Manning stood in the expanded Manning's Hardware, morning light making sawdust motes dance like golden snow around her shoulders. Eleanor's old camera hung from her neck, its weight familiar as breathing.

"Tell me again about the federal agents, grandpa," she said to Noble, her fingers tracing the counter where three generations of Mannings had measured dreams alongside dimensions.

"About Colonel Matthews choosing his mother's memory over his orders."

Noble smiled, watching his granddaughter examine tools with the same careful attention Sarah had once brought to her photographs. Emma possessed her mother's gift for seeing truth in images, but something more: she could help others find balance between their fears and their possibilities.

The store had expanded beyond its original walls, now incorporating the adjacent buildings, where Stanford's bookstore and Jenny's expanded record-keeping operation documented the ongoing work of community transformation. Rosa's original ledger sat in a place of honor, its pages still writing new stories as Cedar Springs welcomed visitors from across the region.

Through the windows, the town demonstrated mature magical integration. Mrs. Chen's daughter, Lisa, managed the bakery, her bread carrying both nutrition and comfort for the steady stream of visitors. Jack Thompson's son Kevin ran the carpentry school, teaching apprentices to read wood grain for both structural integrity and artistic inspiration.

Sarah entered from the back office, where she coordinated the Cedar Springs Institute for Balanced Transformation; her photography documented communities learning to integrate their awakened gifts safely. "Emma," she called, "show them what arrived in the mail."

Emma pulled a manila envelope from behind the counter, extracting photographs taken in distant towns. Each image showed familiar patterns: a bookstore in Portland where customers lingered longer than economics suggested, a café in Ashland where the coffee somehow evoked childhood memories, and an art store in Seattle whose paint brushes inspired their owners to see deep into their imagination.

"They're awakening," Emma said, spreading the photographs across the counter like a map of expanding possibilities. "But faster than we did. Without the foundation we built over time."

Stanford approached from his bookstore section, where customers browsed volumes, whose pages rearranged themselves to display personally relevant passages. His transformation from suppressor to teacher had taken years of patient work, helping other former federal agents understand the difference between protecting communities and controlling them.

"These photographs arrived from seventeen different towns," he said, examining the images. "All places where our normalized communities once existed. The suppression is wearing off."

Jenny emerged from the record-keeping section, her twins organizing customer files alongside transformation documentation. The system tracked both practical purchases and the deeper work of helping visitors integrate their developing abilities.

"The calls started six months ago," Jenny explained, her grandmother's accent stronger when discussing serious matters. "Business owners are reporting equipment behaving strangely. Customers are experiencing unusual sensations. Local officials requesting consultation about managing unexplained phenomena."

Noble felt the familiar pulse where the keys had merged years ago, their rhythm matching his heartbeat. The network Emma's photographs revealed stretched across state lines, connecting communities whose suppressed magic was reasserting itself.

Emma's phone buzzed with messages from strangers whose names she somehow recognized: a teenager in Denver whose grandmother's recipes had started cooking themselves, a librarian in Phoenix whose books whispered their stories after closing hours, a mechanic in Salt Lake City whose repairs lasted longer than physics explained.

"They're scared," Emma said, reading the messages aloud. "They remember what happened before. Federal agents, normalization protocols, communities losing their gifts permanently."

Through the afternoon light streaming across the store, Noble watched visitors from a dozen awakening towns examine tools whose purposes extended beyond simple function.

Cedar Springs had become what his grandfather envisioned: a crossroads where people could learn to traverse safely between ordinary reality and extraordinary possibility.

"The infrastructure exists now," Sarah noted, gesturing toward the institute's training programs, Stanford's counseling services, and Jenny's documentation systems. "We've spent ten years learning how to teach balanced transformation. These communities won't have to discover everything from scratch."

But Emma's most recent photograph showed something concerning: a woman in an expensive suit examining the Portland bookstore with electronic equipment. Victoria Kane, according to Stanford's identification. Integrated Development Corporation, the private company that had purchased properties in all seventeen formerly normalized towns.

"She's not working alone," Stanford said grimly. "Integrated Development represents interests that benefit from keeping communities afraid of their own potential. They'll move to suppress these awakenings before they can stabilize."

Noble walked to the windows overlooking Main Street, where the evening light revealed Cedar Springs in all its evolved complexity. Practical businesses operating efficiently alongside magical services. Regulatory frameworks adapted to accommodate extraordinary circumstances. Federal oversight transformed from suppression into support through Diana Wells' ongoing policy work.

"What happens now?" Emma asked, adjusting Eleanor's camera to capture the golden threads of connection her grandmother's lens revealed, stretching toward distant horizons.

"Now we do what Manning's Hardware has always done," Noble replied, feeling the keys pulse with renewed purpose. "We help people build what needs building. We measure what needs measuring. We keep the doors open between what is and what could be."

"But bigger," Sarah added, recognizing the expansion their work required. "Not one town anymore. A network of communities learning to balance wonder and wisdom together."

Emma raised the camera, its viewfinder showing streams of light connecting Cedar Springs to awakening towns across the region. Through her grandmother's lens, she saw the pattern forming: a web of transformation spreading carefully, supported by experience, guided by hard-won wisdom.

"The second wave is beginning," she announced, her young voice carrying Eleanor's certainty. "And this time, we're ready to help them succeed."

The hardware store's bell chimed as another visitor entered, seeking tools for transformation. But tonight, those tools would serve not one community's needs, but a growing network of towns learning to remember what they had been forced to forget.

Outside, the first stars appeared above Manning's Hardware, their light bending around the building like recognition of work expanding beyond any single crossroads. Cedar Springs had become the seed of something larger: a movement that taught community members how to evolve beyond others' limitations while maintaining the foundations that kept wonder safe.

The real work was beginning.

End of Book One

Coming Soon, Book Two: - **Sacred Networks** *Book Two of the Cedar Springs Chronicles*

The awakening spreads beyond Cedar Springs. Seventeen communities discover their hidden magic simultaneously, but without guidance, their transformations spiral toward chaos. When corporate forces led by Victoria Kane begin systematically acquiring and "normalizing" these towns, twelve-year-old Emma Manning sees the truth through her grandmother's camera: golden threads connect all awakening places in a vast network of human consciousness.

Noble and his team race across the region, teaching communities to balance wonder with wisdom before federal agents shut them down permanently. But Emma's psychic connection to the network comes at a devastating cost. As each town falls to corporate suppression, the remaining communities feel the loss like severed nerves.

The choice becomes stark: fight separately and fall, or risk everything by merging their consciousness into something humanity has never attempted. Success means evolutionary breakthrough. Failure means the permanent suppression of human potential.

Some awakenings are worth any price. Others demand we become more than we ever thought possible.

The network is calling. Will you answer?

THE WISDOM SUMMARIES

Chapter 1: The Well-Lit Path "The systems we build for safety can become the barriers preventing our growth. What serves us in one season may confine us in the next."

Chapter 2: When the Light Shifts "Loss creates space for what wants to emerge. When familiar voices fall silent, we finally hear what our deeper self has been trying to say."

Chapter 3: What Can't Be Measured "Grief strips away everything nonessential, revealing what actually matters. Our most profound discoveries happen when our old measuring tools prove inadequate."

Chapter 4: The Space Between "What appears threatening in our darkness often carries the invitation to expand beyond our current limitations. Guides rarely look like what we expect."

Chapter 5: Crossroads "Every crossroads demands we release who we've been to discover who we're becoming. The path forward only reveals itself when we stop clinging to the path behind."

Chapter 6: Shadow and Light "Those who resist our transformation often mirror our own internal conflicts. Understanding their fear can illuminate the courage required for our next steps."

Chapter 7: The Evidence of Fear "The structures meant to protect us can become the prisons that limit us. True security comes from learning to navigate change skillfully rather than avoiding it entirely."

Chapter 8: The Father's Truth "Our wounds often mark where our greatest gifts are trying to emerge. What breaks us open creates space for what wants to be born through us."

Chapter 9: The Price of Wonder "Awakening requires not just the courage to transform but the commitment to sustain transformation against forces that prefer us unchanged."

Chapter 10: Divided Ground "Home isn't a destination but a way of being that honors both our roots and our growth. We find our place by becoming authentically ourselves."

Chapter 11: When Ancient Power... "Crisis reveals whether our transformation has deep roots or shallow soil. What survives the storm proves worthy of trust."

Chapter 12: The Evidence of Truth "Sometimes we must risk everything we've built to preserve what we've become. Truth demands we choose it over comfort, growth over safety."

Chapter 13: A Town Divided "Division shows us where healing is needed most. What splits communities often reveals where integration must happen within ourselves."

Chapter 14: Against Orders "The journey toward truth requires us to abandon positions that no longer serve life's expansion. Courage is choosing love over loyalty to limiting systems."

Chapter 15: Cleansing Power of Light "Our deepest victories happen when we demonstrate that growth and stability can strengthen each other. Transformation proves its worth by creating rather than destroying."

Chapter 16: The Teaching Begins "What we learn for ourselves becomes a gift we offer others. Our personal healing contributes to collective awakening when shared with wisdom."

Epilogue: "Our individual transformations become seeds for others' awakenings. The sacred crossroads we navigate personally create pathways for communities to follow."

A MESSAGE FROM THE AUTHOR

Sacred Crossroads came out of a period in my life when the things I once relied on: certainty, identity, and long-held ideas about success... quietly stopped working.

In the autumn of 2023, I experienced a full-on spiritual awakening. Over the course of a few minutes, I felt as if I was one with everything, including the Divine. The awe of seeing from this new perspective was overwhelming, as everything I thought I knew came apart, and suddenly my life lacked relevance or meaning. I realized that I had to start over with just about everything.

The roles and labels I'd lived by no longer fit. Milestones that once mattered stopped having any value to me, and for months, I asked myself, "What's wrong?" But the answers weren't there.

I finally realized I was asking the wrong question. Instead, I wondered, *What now?* What remained was a stillness that felt unfamiliar and... uncomfortable... a space I would later understand as the void.

I had no guidance, I had no teacher, but I kept going deeper. Instead of rushing to fill that space, I chose to stay with it. I let go of the need to immediately explain what was happening or turn it into something useful. I sat for weeks in intermittent silence, staring at the ocean, waiting for direction, connection, but nothing specific surfaced.

Over time, something shifted. In the absence of noise and certainty, a deeper sense of knowing began to surface, not in the form of answers but as recognition. This book grew out of that time. I journaled for months, trying to find threads of understanding; asking, "Where am I?" and "What Now?"

Then a spark. A message from the void, the instructions were simple. Start writing. And I did.

While *Sacred Crossroads* is a work of fiction, it's closely tied to my own inner journey. The make-believe town of Cedar Springs, the character of Noble Manning, and the events that unfold reflect what it feels like to stand at a threshold, when the life you've built no longer quite fits, and a new way of seeing begins to take shape.

I wrote to explore myself, using "story" as a way to reach places that explanation can't.

As the book took form, I realized I wasn't alone in this experience. I met others who found themselves at similar crossroads: after loss, disruption, or a quieter awakening that doesn't come with a clear roadmap. If you've found yourself questioning what once felt solid, this book was written with you in mind.

Today, my work continues to explore that space where the practical and the unseen meet. Through writing and conversation, I stay honest about what it means to move through change without rushing past it.

I don't see *Sacred Crossroads* as a book of answers, but as an invitation... to pause, to notice what's shifting, and to trust what's beginning to emerge.

If this story resonated on any level, I'd love to hear from you.

You can reach me at **AuthorMitchRusso@gmail.com**.

You'll also find additional resources, including the Wisdom Summaries PDF, Book club study materials, and news about my local bookstore visits, podcast episodes, and TV appearances, at **SacredCrossroadsBook.com**.

With Love,

Mitch Russo

For Book Clubs & Reading Groups

If you're reading *Sacred Crossroads* with your book club or reading group, request the complete Book Club Discussion Kit. The kit includes expanded discussion questions, thematic exploration exercises, and additional author insights to enrich your conversations. You can request your kit or request a virtual author visit to your book club by contacting Author MitchRusso@gmail.com.

www.ingramcontent.com/pod-product-compliance
Lightning Source LLC
Chambersburg PA
CBHW040331020826
48978CB00013BC/1133